05/14

Home Is Beyond the Mountains

Home
Is
Beyond
the
Mountains

Celia Barker Lottridge

GROUNDWOOD BOOKS
HOUSE OF ANANSI PRESS
TORONTO   BERKELEY

Groundwood Books / House of Anansi Press
110 Spadina Avenue, Suite 801, Toronto, Ontario M5V 2K4
or c/o Publishers Group West
1700 Fourth Street, Berkeley, CA 94710

We acknowledge for their financial support of our publishing program the Canada
Council for the Arts, the Government of Canada through the Canada Book Fund
(CBF) and the Ontario Arts Council.

 Canada Council   Conseil des Arts
for the Arts   du Canada

 ONTARIO ARTS COUNCIL
CONSEIL DES ARTS DE L'ONTARIO

This book was written with the support of an Ontario Arts Council
Works in Progress Grant.

Library and Archives Canada Cataloguing in Publication
Lottridge, Celia B. (Celia Barker)
Home is beyond the mountains / Celia Barker Lottridge.
ISBN 978-0-88899-932-0 (bound).–ISBN 978-0-88899-949-8 (pbk.)
I. Title.
PS8573.O855H65 2010   jC813'.54   C2009-906085-X

Cover photos of Hamadan Orphanage courtesy of Jane Montgomery
Maps drawn by Leon Grek
Design by Michael Solomon

Groundwood Books is committed to protecting our natural environment.
As part of our efforts, this book is printed on paper that contains 100%
post-consumer recycled fibers, is acid-free and is processed chlorine-free.

Printed and bound in Canada

For

Louise Shedd Barker

and

Marion Seary

who inspired me with their stories and
encouraged me with their listening

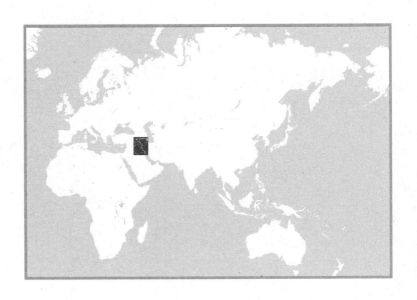

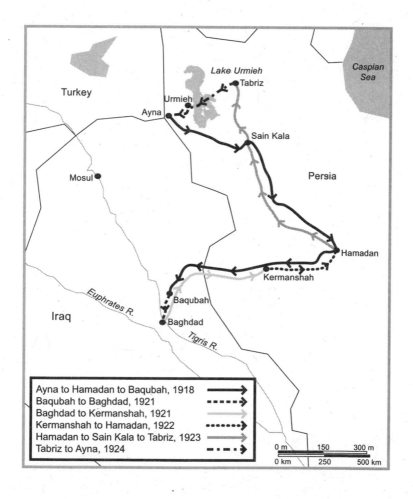

Ayna to Hamadan to Baqubah, 1918	→
Baqubah to Baghdad, 1921	→
Baghdad to Kermanshah, 1921	→
Kermanshah to Hamadan, 1922	→
Hamadan to Sain Kala to Tabriz, 1923	→
Tabriz to Ayna, 1924	→

ONE

No Safe Place

Ayna, Persia
July 1918

A SOUND, a very quiet sound, woke Samira.

What was it? She listened but she kept her eyes tightly closed, hoping she could drift back into sleep.

"We always hear noises when we sleep on the roof," she told herself. "It must be the donkey stamping its hoof, or Papa snoring." She put out her hand and touched her little sister, Maryam, who was sleeping beside her. Maybe it was just a dream.

Then she heard it again. Metal clinking against metal and then a voice, whispering.

Samira sat up. The sky was clear and black. There was no moon, but the stars gave enough light that she could see Mama lying on her sleeping mat on the other side of Maryam. Beyond her was Papa and then her brother, Benyamin. They were all sleeping quietly.

She listened, holding her breath. Where had the sound come from?

There was no more clinking but the whispering came again.

Samira pushed her thin summer quilt aside and stood up. The clay floor was rough under her bare feet as she silently crossed the flat roof.

She was sure now. The whispering was coming from the

Celia Barker Lottridge

garden behind the house. Boys from a nearby village sometimes sneaked into Ayna to steal a few ripe melons. Well, she would catch them this time.

There was a wall around the edge of the roof, but by standing on tiptoe Samira could see over it and over the wall that surrounded the village. The garden was on a hillside so she could see the almond tree and the rows of peppers and eggplants and the tangle of melon vines. Among the melons were three figures dressed in bulky clothes and wearing strange peaked caps.

No village boy wore such a cap, and these were not boys. They were men.

Then Samira saw a glint of starlight on something shiny. There it was again.

It was the blade of a knife. The man was lifting a melon and cutting it from the vine. He lowered it to the ground and its pale round shape disappeared.

"They are thieves," thought Samira. "That man is cutting melons and putting them in a sack."

The man stood up and lifted the sack to his shoulder, and Samira saw that he had a rifle strapped to his back. The knife in his hand clinked against the rifle barrel. That was the sound that had wakened her.

Samira turned to call for Papa but suddenly a hand gripped her around the ankle. She looked down and saw her father crouched beside her. He let go of her ankle and pulled her down and put his hand over her mouth.

He leaned close and whispered so softly that she could hardly hear him. "Be quiet. They must not know you saw them."

Samira tried to open her mouth to ask a question, but Papa held his hand firm and whispered again, "I'll tell you in the morning. Don't stand up."

She nodded and he let her go. She crawled over to her sleeping mat. Papa pulled the quilt up around her and patted her on the shoulder.

"Sleep," he said without making a sound. Then he moved away on his hands and knees.

Samira reached for Maryam and pulled her close. For a long time she lay with her eyes open, listening. But it was quiet now, and after a while she fell asleep.

When she woke, she was alone. She sat up and looked around the roof that covered her house and the connected house where Uncle Avram lived with his family. On warm nights both families liked to sleep on the roof, out in the fresh air.

But now the sun was high in the sky. Everyone else would have drunk their tea and eaten their morning bread and cheese. Benyamin had probably gone to school, and Papa would be out in the garden.

Suddenly Samira remembered the dark figures stealing melons. She scrambled up, pulled on her skirt and blouse and climbed quickly down the ladder.

In the house it was bread-baking day. Mama was kneading dough in a big bowl while Maryam played with her doll as she always did while Mama worked.

But this morning Papa was there, too. He had a basket in his arms. It was empty except for one pale green melon.

"Samira," he said. "I let you sleep because you were disturbed by the men in the garden last night. Do you remember anything about them?"

Samira closed her eyes, trying to see again the figures in the starlight.

"There were three of them," she said. "They wore stiff jackets and caps that covered their ears. They had knives and they were cutting melons." She opened her eyes. "And they had rifles. Who were they, Papa?"

"Uniforms and guns," said Papa. "They were soldiers, not ordinary thieves. I've heard that deserters from the Turkish army have come through the mountains into Persia. They don't want to fight in the war anymore but they don't mind stealing. They were hungry and our melons are just getting ripe. This is the only one they missed."

"What if they come again?" said Samira.

"We must stay quiet and be watchful. I told Benyamin to come straight home after school. No one should be wandering around the countryside. I'm going out to the garden to pick whatever is ripe or nearly ripe. If the soldiers do come back they won't find much to steal."

He handed the melon to Samira and left.

Mama set the bowl of bread dough to one side and said, "Get some bread and cheese for your breakfast and take Maryam next door to play with Ester and Negris. Sahra will come soon to bake bread with me, so I'm going to uncover the oven now and build up the fire."

The oven was a round hole dug into the earthen floor of the house, lined with smooth clay and covered with a lid. The fire burned at the bottom and most days an iron pot filled with the day's stew was set to cook down inside the oven with the top almost closed. But on bread-baking day the cover was left off. It would be too easy for Maryam to stumble and fall in.

Aunt Sahra and Mama would pat the bread dough into big thin ovals. Mama would slap the ovals onto the hot sides of the oven. In just a few minutes the bread would be brown and bubbling. Aunt Sahra would lift it off with wooden tongs. By the end of the baking there would be a pile of lawash flatbread, enough to last both families for a week or more.

Samira took Maryam out onto the terrace. There was an oven out there, too, and in the summer Mama and Aunt Sahra always baked bread outside. But today things were different.

Maryam tugged at her hand and the two girls walked to the next wooden door and into a house that was almost exactly like theirs. There was just one room, square with whitewashed walls. The only furniture was a big carved chest where sleeping mats and quilts and clothes were stored. The floor was covered with beautiful rugs and there were cushions to sit on, though the children usually sat on the floor.

Aunt Sahra was busy tidying up. As always she moved quickly and talked even faster.

"I want you girls to play in the house today," she said. "There are too many strangers around." So Samira knew that she had heard about the soldiers in the garden.

When all the breakfast crumbs had been brushed away and the tea glasses washed, she looked at the four girls.

"Ester and Samira, I want you to take good care of your

little sisters," she said. "If anything strange happens, call me at once."

She didn't pick up her basket and leave until Ester nodded and Samira said, "Yes, Aunt Sahra."

Samira wondered what her aunt was thinking. Bread-baking day was always the same. But it would be easy to let Aunt Sahra and Mama know if anything did happen. There was a hole in the wall between the two houses. It was just above Samira's head and big enough for her hand to fit through. Most of the time the hole was blocked by a roll of cloth, but the cloth could be removed. Then people on either side of the wall could talk to each other.

The hole was open now. They were not really alone.

"Let's play school," said Ester. She was seven, just two years younger than Samira. Like Samira she longed to go to school, but so far no teacher for the girls had come to the village. The Assyrian Orthodox Church ran the boys' school, and the priest had promised that one day the girls would have a school, too.

Samira and Ester thought they would probably be grown up before this happened.

Sometimes they peeked into the schoolroom next to the church, so they knew that the teacher should have a chair and a table and big board to write on. The pupils should have little boards and chalk so that they could copy what the teacher wrote. And there should be a book for the teacher and some pages with writing on them so that the pupils could practice reading.

All of this was easy to pretend. Samira was the oldest so she was the teacher. She sat on the fattest cushion. Ester and

Negris, who was five, were good pupils. They sat quietly on the rug and listened to the teacher and practiced writing with their fingers on flat pieces of wood. Maryam was only three and she was not a very good pupil, though sometimes she would sit with her doll and listen to a story. Today she wanted to sit very close to Negris. Maybe she had heard something in the night, too.

Samira stood up and turned to the wall behind her cushion.

"Today I have something special to teach you," she said. "Last Sunday when we were waiting for Mama and Papa to come home from the church, Benyamin taught me the first three letters of the Syriac alphabet. He promised to teach me more, but this is the beginning."

She pointed at the wall.

"This is the board where I will write the letters. Watch closely. This is *alap*, the first letter." With her finger she made a straight bottom line with a dot above it and a curved line that connected the dot to the line.

Of course, her finger made no mark on the wall, but she hoped the little girls would get the idea. She drew the letter again and then stopped.

Through the hole in the wall she heard Aunt Sahra's voice clearly. It was high and fierce.

"Even if you do go, I'm staying here. Or I'll go to the city with the girls. But army or no army I'm not going far until Avram comes home."

Avram was Sahra's husband. He had set off on a long journey to the city of Tabriz across Lake Urmieh to inquire about taking his whole family to America. He said Persia wasn't safe anymore.

Samira suddenly realized that the other girls were staring at her, waiting for her to draw another letter. Sitting on the floor, they hadn't heard Aunt Sahra's voice. And now Samira couldn't hear it, either. Her mother must have reminded Aunt Sahra that walls have ears. Now there was no sound of voices, only the slap of the bread against the wall of the oven.

"You're the teacher, Samira," Maryam said. "You have to talk."

Samira blinked.

"Yes," she said. "I was just thinking about the second letter. It's *beet* and it looks like this."

When the bread was all baked, Aunt Sahra came back. She set down her basket filled with a stack of lawash and tidied up the cushions the girls had used, just as she always did. But she was so quiet that all four girls became quiet, too.

Samira wanted to ask Aunt Sahra what she meant when she said, "Army or no army." But she didn't.

Suddenly her aunt noticed that her nieces were still there.

"My goodness," she said. "You and Maryam should go home now, Samira. There is work to be done and your mother needs your help."

Then she remembered to hug them quickly before she opened the door and gave them a little push toward home.

AT HOME the floor was covered with baskets of eggplants and squash and peppers. Papa had done just what he'd said he would do. He had picked everything in the garden.

Mama was standing among the baskets shaking her head.

"We have to cut up all these vegetables so we can spread them to dry tomorrow," she said.

"The squash are so small," said Samira.

"I know. It's too soon to pick any of this. But we have to keep it safe or we won't have enough to eat in the winter. Now go and get a knife so we can get started."

Samira nodded and went to get a small knife from the shelf. She had questions but she knew this was not the time to ask them.

By suppertime the baskets were filled with neatly sliced vegetables, and the stew that had been cooking in the oven was ready to eat. The family sat in a circle around the big clay bowl and took turns scooping up the savory stew with torn pieces of fresh lawash.

They were all quiet. In summer they usually ate on the terrace, and the children finished quickly so they could play with their friends before darkness sent everyone to bed. Tonight no one wanted to move even when the bowl was empty.

At last Benyamin spoke. "We didn't have lessons today at school. Instead our teacher told us that we must remember that we are Assyrians and we have been here in Persia for centuries. All through history we have had our villages and our orthodox churches and our own language, Syriac. No matter what happens we must remember that we belong here."

Papa said, "Your teacher is right. But the Turkish army doesn't care that this is our home. They are fighting in a big war with many countries and they are using the war as an excuse to cross into Persia to take our land. The British army might want to protect us but it is far away to the south. Persia is not in the war and it has no army so there is nothing to stop these soldiers from driving us from our villages. From what I hear, the soldiers are in the mountains now, attacking the villages there. We may be safer because we are near the city of Urmieh. There are people in the city from America and from France who want to protect us. Maybe they can help. We have to watch and wait."

When it grew dark Papa said it was not safe to sleep on the roof, so the family spent a stuffy night in the house. They all woke up very early.

As soon as they had eaten, Mama sent Samira to lay clean cloths on the roof. Together they would spread the cut vegetables to dry. Later they would store them in the umbar, the cellar under the terrace, to be used for soups and stews all winter.

When she got to the roof, Samira took a minute to watch Benyamin and the other village boys run down the street on their way to school.

She was just turning away when she heard the sound of galloping horses. She listened.

People in the village did not have horses. Their donkeys and mules walked slowly, carrying heavy loads. Galloping horses meant strangers.

In no time at all, the narrow road outside the village wall was filled with men on horseback. They wore turbans and had cartridge belts slung across their chests and sabers stuck in their belts. Samira knew they were Kurds — mountain people who often came through the village selling rugs and sometimes raiding the orchards and flocks. People told many stories about the Kurds — how they would stop travelers and take all their money and belongings or, sometimes, show them a better way through the mountains.

But where were they going today, galloping so fast?

The sound sent the boys dodging back into their houses or diving into small gaps between the buildings. They were taking no chances. The Kurds might come through the gate in the village wall.

But the horsemen did not look left or right. They galloped past Ayna and were gone. Benyamin came home to tell Mama and Papa that he was all right.

Papa said, "You were right to hide. Some of the Kurds are helping the Turkish soldiers. They've probably been told they'll be given some land. It's not a good sign when Kurds come past without wanting food or money from the village. I think something is about to happen."

Papa was right. The next day someone hammered at the door while the family was eating their evening meal.

Papa went to the door but he didn't open it.

"Who are you?" he said in a loud voice.

A voice answered, "Your cousin Youel."

Papa opened the door. He looked for a long moment at the dusty man who stood on the doorstep.

"It is you, Youel," he said, and he embraced the man and pulled him inside.

Benyamin stepped forward to greet Youel. Mama and Samira waited quietly for him to greet them.

When the greetings were over Papa said, "You have come a long way. Drink some tea and tell us why you are here. Then you can eat."

Youel drank his tea in one long gulp. Then he said, "You must leave Ayna at once. The Turkish army is moving in this direction, burning the mountain villages as they come. The Assyrian people are running to save their lives. So are the Armenians. There's no safe place for us in our land. I'm going to join with other Assyrian and Armenian men to try to stop the soldiers or slow them down, but you have a family. You must all go now."

Samira was surprised when Mama spoke. Usually when visitors came she sat quietly and listened, but now she said, "Where can we go? If we can't stay where we have always lived, where can we go?"

"You must head toward Hamadan. The British army is there. Those soldiers will protect you."

Mama shook her head as if she couldn't understand what he was saying.

Papa frowned. "I have heard that a mule caravan takes twenty-five days or more to travel from Urmieh to Hamadan. And the road through the mountains is very rough, they say."

"You have to go," said Youel. "That army will come and steal what they can and burn the rest. They don't care who they kill, either."

After that Papa and Youel went to talk on the roof. Samira and Benyamin looked at each other. They knew that the men didn't want them to hear what they were saying.

Mama tidied away the spoons and tea glasses, but she kept glancing at the ceiling as if she wanted to hear the men talking.

Samira was thinking of one word Youel had said. Hamadan.

Where was Hamadan? She decided to ask Benyamin. He went to school and she knew that on the wall of the schoolroom there was a big map of Persia. Hamadan must be on that map.

"Benyamin," she said. "This Hamadan where our cousin says we should go, is it a city?"

"Yes, it's a big city. If we go south over the mountains and down into the plain, we'll come to Hamadan. But it will take a long time. When I went to the sheep market in Urmieh with Papa we went just a tiny distance on the map, less than the width of my little finger, but it took us all day."

Samira nodded. She remembered how tired Benyamin had been when he came back from that journey to the city.

Benyamin sighed a deep sigh. "On the map Hamadan is three or four hands away from Ayna." He shook his head and said no more.

Youel was gone before daylight. Papa went with him a little way down the road before he said goodbye.

He returned to wake the family. "Youel was right. People running from the danger are already coming past the village."

Samira and Benyamin went up to the roof to look. There they were, people coming from the western mountains, all going the same direction, toward the south. Some rode horses laden with bundles, others had big oxcarts that carried the whole family and their household goods, but most walked beside small carts pulled by donkeys.

Papa went out to the road with a jug of water and some bread. Samira came down from the roof and stood beside him. They offered the refreshment to a family walking beside a cart pulled by a mule. It was overflowing with bags of grain, rolled-up rugs and baskets of vegetables. An old, old woman rode on top, staring straight ahead.

Papa spoke to the man of the family. "How long have you been traveling?" he asked.

"For three days now. Our village is in the mountains, and the soldiers came and burned the church. They searched our houses for our young men, but they had gone to hide in caves. The soldiers were angry so they smashed whatever they could and threw dirt in the well. Then they went away to find another village. We left the next day."

"Where will you go?"

"The British army is fighting the Turkish army. We'll walk until we come to the British army. They will protect us."

"That will be a long walk," said Papa.

"Yes. But here we have no one to defend us. We have to go."

Papa filled the water jug the man carried. He took Samira's hand in his and held it while they watched the man give his wife and his three children and the old grandmother water to drink before they traveled on.

In the house Mama was sitting very still with Maryam in her arms. She pulled Samira down beside her and held both of her daughters close. Benyamin came in and stood beside Papa.

Samira could see dark thoughts cross her father's face.

"We are threatened just as those people are threatened," he said at last. "We can't stay here."

"I know," said Mama. "We must leave. Maybe we should go to the city, to Urmieh, with my sister."

"Sahra wants to wait for Avram," said Papa. "I pray she will be safe. But they say the city is already full of refugees. There is sickness and starvation. I think we'll be safer on the road."

Mama nodded. She let go of Samira and set Maryam on her feet.

"All right, children," she said. "Find your extra clothes, and I'll need help getting some things from the umbar."

Papa said, "I'll bring the cart. We'll load up today and start out tomorrow."

The day passed in a swirl of deciding what to take, packing up, trying not to forget anything, worrying about what would happen to things left behind.

When Samira finally lay down to sleep she could feel the house around her. She had never slept anywhere but in this room or on the roof above it.

Tomorrow she would be somewhere far away.

THEN IT was morning, and before she had time to be properly awake, Samira was walking beside Mama, away from Ayna.

She looked back through the gate in the village wall. There was the house she had lived in all her life. Already it looked lonely and abandoned. Aunt Sahra and Ester and Negris stood waving. They had little bundles of clothes beside them, ready for their journey to the city.

"How can we go without them?" Samira thought. But she said nothing. Mama was already crying.

Samira looked around. They had joined a great procession of frightened people — men, women and children with their carts and their animals. Families from Ayna were mixed in with people who had already walked for days. Some were silent. Others talked and called to their friends.

"I can't understand what those people ahead of us are saying," she said to Mama.

Mama wiped her eyes with the ends of her scarf and listened. "They're speaking Armenian," she said. "We Assyrians are not the only people who must run away."

By nightfall they had traveled farther than Samira had ever gone before. Maryam was asleep on top of the bundles in the wagon, and Samira felt as if she would fall asleep walking if they didn't stop.

"We'll camp here for the night," Papa said. They had come to an open field dotted with little groups of people. Some had built small fires and spread out rugs or quilts to lie on. Others were preparing to lie on the bare ground.

Mama lifted Maryam down from the cart, and Samira spread out the one rug they had brought from the house. It was worn but it looked welcoming. The most beautiful rugs were at home in Ayna, hidden in the umbar where they might be safe.

Papa built a little fire and poured water into the kettle from the jug he carried. They had tea with sugar in it and bread with cheese and some pieces of dried pepper from the umbar. Samira remembered all the eggplant and squash they had left drying on the roof.

"I hope the birds eat it all before thieves get it," she thought just before she fell asleep.

For a while the days had a pattern. They woke very early and ate dried fruit before they started out. Maryam rode in the wagon and Papa and Benyamin walked beside the donkey. Samira and Mama followed.

The land was dry and hot in the summer sun. Dust hung thick in the air, stirred up by all the feet and hooves that were walking, walking. Whenever they came to a river they scooped up water to carry for themselves and the donkey.

Papa kept track of the days, and when Sunday came the family took time to stand in a circle and say a prayer together.

When another Sunday came Papa said, "We still have food to eat and a little grain for the donkey, so we can be thankful."

Looking up the rocky slope that lay ahead of them, Samira only wished that she could sleep under a roof and eat something besides dry bread and a few dates. She did not feel very thankful. Still, she said the prayer.

A few days later a wheel of the cart broke and there was no way to fix it.

"We have to go on with what we can carry," said Papa. "We'll let the donkey go. We have nothing to feed him and perhaps he'll find food for himself."

Samira had no love for the donkey. He was stubborn and would nip her with his teeth if he got a chance, but she wept to see him wandering away into the hills.

Papa and Benyamin took everything out of the cart and spread it on the ground.

"Benyamin and I will carry the food and the tools," said Papa.

"I'll wrap some clothes in the quilt and strap it to my back," said Samira. "The quilt might keep us from freezing at night."

Celia Barker Lottridge

Mama said nothing. She would carry Maryam, who could only walk a little distance now.

As they went on, Samira saw more and more piles of household goods that had been left by people whose carts had broken or whose animals had died. Iron pots and pottery bowls, rugs and quilts and stacks of clothes. Even sacks of grain. None of that mattered as much as getting away to safety.

Now there was no pattern to their days. They struggled up steep mountainsides and down again. Samira's feet were sore and blistered. When they had to rest they ate some dried fruit or stale bread. They drank water whenever they crossed a stream and they slept when it was too dark to see the stones in the road.

Samira stopped noticing anything but the path in front of her, but sometimes, among all the bundles and dead animals that lay along the path, she could not help seeing a narrow pile of earth where someone had been buried, or even a body wrapped in pieces of cloth and left behind.

She asked Papa why these people had died and he said, "Some were not strong enough for this journey. Now they say a fever has broken out." His eyes went to Maryam who hardly ever walked now and had grown so thin that Mama had no trouble carrying her all day. Samira felt a new knot of fear in her chest.

One day they came to a river too deep to wade across. There was a bridge strung on ropes between the high banks. It was narrow and made of small sticks that looked as if they might break under a traveler's weight. It swayed above the rushing water, and even before she stepped on the bridge Samira felt herself sway, too.

"Look at that big rock on the other side of the river," said Benyamin sharply. "Don't look at the water." He took hold of the strap that held her pack to her back. "I'll catch you if you fall. Don't look down."

"If I fall, you'll fall, too," thought Samira, but she didn't say it out loud. She could feel her brother behind her as she clung to the ropes at the sides of the bridge and stepped from one stick to the next.

When they both stood on the hard earth at the other side of the river, she knew that they had crossed safely because they were together

Mama and Papa caught up with them, and Samira forgot her relief. Papa was carrying Maryam. When he laid her gently on the ground she didn't try to get up. Samira could see that her sister's face was flushed and her eyes were bright with fever.

Papa put his hand on her forehead.

"She's very hot," he said, and his voice was deep with sadness. Mama knelt and took Maryam in her arms and looked helplessly around her.

Back in their village there were wise people who knew of herbs that might help a little girl with a fever. Or a doctor might come from the city to see her. Here there was nothing.

They stayed by the river all day and bathed Maryam with cool water. Benyamin made a little tent with the quilt to shelter her from the glaring sun. People coming by offered them water and a little food, but no one could give real help.

When night came Samira fell asleep, exhausted by sorrow.

Celia Barker Lottridge

She woke in the early dawn and turned to look at her small sister, but Maryam lay perfectly still, and Mama's shawl covered her face.

At home when someone died, there was weeping and wailing. The priest came and mourned with the family. There was a funeral in the church.

Here none of this could happen, except the weeping. Even that was hard. It was so strange to be here on this wild mountainside by a dusty road when something so terrible had happened. Samira couldn't feel what was the right thing to do.

But Papa said, "We will bury her properly. We will dig a grave for Maryam."

In his pack he had a knife with a strong blade. Now he used it to chip a hole in the hard earth. Benyamin scooped the dirt away with his hands. They labored together until the grave was dug. Then they laid small Maryam, wrapped in her mother's shawl, carefully in the ground.

Mama had hardly said anything this whole time, but now she said a prayer.

"Lord, we give our daughter and our sister, Maryam, into your hands. Take care of her and love her. Amen."

All the time they were burying Maryam, people were passing by on the road. Some bowed their heads but no one stopped. So many had died that everyone who passed was carrying sadness and must still go on. Samira and her family stood around the grave for only a few minutes. Then they, too, had to walk on.

After a few more days the straggling line of refugees came out into a wide valley. The walking was easier and for a short time the people felt relief, but then word began to spread that Turkish soldiers were coming.

"They're looking for men who were part of the Assyrian and Armenian forces that protected us as we set out," one old man told Papa. "But the war has taken their senses and they see us all as the enemy."

There was no place to hide in that open land and so people just kept going. They could see that there was a narrow pass leading into the next mountains. If they could reach that place they might be able to find shelter.

Then a horseman came galloping. He called out, "Soldiers are coming. They're shooting at the men and the boys. You must hurry."

Samira's mother looked at her son and her husband. "You can go faster without Samira and me. Go ahead. Hide in the mountains. We will find you when we reach the mountains."

There was no time to talk. Papa touched Mama and Samira on the shoulder.

"We'll wait for you at the next river," he said. Then he and Benyamin began to run.

The soldiers came. They came on horseback, galloping and firing their rifles into the air. When they saw a man or a tall boy, they shot at him. Some they hit and some they missed. They rode all the way along the long line of people and then disappeared into the mountains.

Samira did not look around. If she did she would see men and boys, hurt and dying. She looked ahead to the mountains, just as she had looked at the rock when she was crossing the swaying bridge.

Mama and Samira reached the mountain pass. They kept

Celia Barker Lottridge

going, looking always for Papa and Benyamin, but they didn't find them. There was nothing to do but walk, stopping to sleep when tiredness overtook them.

One night they came to a flat field where many people had stopped for the night.

"It's good to be among so many," Mama said, and they rolled themselves in the quilt and went to sleep.

Samira was wakened by the sound of a voice. It was a small voice and it wavered, but she could hear what it was saying. "Mama, Mama."

Samira sat up and looked around. Half a moon was shining, and all around her she could see people lying as if they had dropped from exhaustion. No one else seemed to hear the faint voice, but Samira kept searching with her eyes until she saw a little figure wandering unsteadily among the sleeping people.

It was a little girl, she was sure. A little girl who had lost her mother in this nameless place.

She was just thinking that she should tell Mama when her mother opened her eyes.

"Maryam?" she said. "Maryam, is that you?"

Samira couldn't breathe. What could she say? But then her mother was sitting up.

"That child is lost," she said and stood up. She made her way between the sleepers until she came to the little girl. Then she knelt and said, "I'll help you find your mama."

She took the little girl by the hand and they walked together. Samira could see her mother bending to talk to the child and knew she was asking, "Is that your mother there? Or there?"

Samira found herself praying without thinking about it.

"Let her be alive," she prayed. "Let her mother be alive."

It seemed that she had been praying for a long time but maybe it was only a few minutes when one of the sleeping people suddenly stood up as if she had been pulled from the ground. She reached out her arms and the little girl ran into them.

Samira's mother watched for just a moment. Then she came back to Samira and put her arms around her.

"She is with her mother now," she said. And then she lay down and went to sleep. Samira slept, too,

In the morning Samira and Mama smiled at each other remembering the little girl, but as the days went on Mama grew weak and feverish. Each night Samira tried to find a sheltered place for them to sleep, and as they walked she let her mother lean on her. She didn't know what else to do.

She was wondering how much longer her own strength would last when a woman came by in a small wagon pulled by a mule. She stopped when she saw Mama stumbling and came over to her. Samira saw that she was not Assyrian, but she spoke Syriac to Samira.

"Your mother is very ill," she said to Samira. "I'll take you to the next camping place. There may be a doctor there. I'm from the American mission in Urmieh. We hoped we could help on this terrible journey and sometimes we can do a little. Come. We'll make your mother as comfortable as we can."

In the wagon Samira could do nothing but sit beside Mama and hold her hand. All day they jolted over a rocky road, and Samira tried to talk to Mama, to tell her that the journey would end soon. But her mother didn't answer, and as the last rays of the sun slanted across the rough land, Samira saw that her mother had died.

She crawled up to the front of the wagon and spoke to the kind woman.

"My mother is gone," she said.

The woman stopped the mule and went to Samira's mother.

"Yes, she is gone," she said quietly. "Oh, my poor child." She put her arm around Samira for a moment. Then she said, "We'll find a place to lay her to rest." She took off the shawl she was wearing and wrapped it around Mama.

Samira got back into the wagon and sat by her mother as the woman drove a short way until they reached a place where a river must flow after a rain. Now there was just a narrow stream between steep rocky banks.

The woman said, "We must leave your mother here above the river. Maybe some day we can come back and bury her as we should. Perhaps you can remember the name of the village nearby. It is called Sain Kala."

Two men came with a shovel and made a grave. When Mama was buried, the woman went with Samira to gather rocks to put on the grave so that animals couldn't dig it up.

She stood beside Samira and bowed her head and said a small prayer. Then she said, "Amen."

"Amen," said Samira. After that she did not speak.

It was dark now and the kind woman found her another wagon to ride in the next day, explaining that she must go back along the road to find others who needed help. Later other people took her into wagons or walked with her, but Samira didn't know who they were or where she was on the journey.

At every river she looked for Papa and Benyamin, but they were never there.

Samira did not count the days, but afterwards she heard that the long, terrible journey took twenty-eight days. Or thirty. No one knew for sure, but at last the people who were walking came to a place where there were soldiers and tents. Samira could hear voices around her saying "Hamadan" and "British army." She stopped walking and stood still.

A man in a uniform came up to her. Samira thought he must be a British soldier. He gave her a piece of strange hard bread and a tin cup of water. When she had drunk the water he took the cup and gave her a handful of raisins.

Then he said, "Syriac?"

Samira nodded. Yes, she spoke Syriac.

The man took her by her shoulders and said two words. They meant, "Your people." Then he pointed her toward a large group of people under some chinar trees. They seemed very far away, but the soldier gave her a little push and turned to someone else with his bread and raisins.

As Samira walked toward the group she saw many women and children and only a few men sitting in little groups, just waiting. They were so dusty that they almost seemed to be part of the earth. A few stood and watched the soldiers send one person after another toward them.

As someone new approached, one of these people would call out a question.

Soon Samira could hear the words. "What village?"

She stopped, confused. A woman came toward her. She

Celia Barker Lottridge

looked very old and her clothes were so dirty that Samira could not see the color of the fabric. But her eyes were bright and she spoke kindly.

"Dear child," she said. "You are alone. Can you tell me what village you come from? Perhaps there is someone else from that village with us here."

Samira thought of her family. None of them were here. But she could say the name of the village.

She whispered, "Ayna."

"Ayna," said the woman. "There was someone saying that name." Suddenly she shouted, "Ayna! Ayna!" making Samira jump.

Immediately the crowd of people began to ripple and murmur. "Ayna, Ayna, where is that boy? A boy. You know, a boy who said Ayna."

The words flowed around Samira like water, and then she saw a boy coming out of the crowd. She was startled at how tall he was and how thin but she knew he was Benyamin. He came to her and, for the first time she could remember, he put his arms around her.

"Samira, Samira," he said. "You are here. But, Mama. Where is Mama?"

"She couldn't walk anymore and she died, Benyamin. She died." She didn't want to ask but she had to. "Papa?"

"I don't know." Benyamin stopped hugging her and stood looking at the ground. "The soldiers came. We hid in a gully but I was smaller and Papa said I could fit in the narrow place at the end so I squeezed in. I heard the soldiers shouting and clanking their weapons but I couldn't see anything and when it was quiet I came out. No one was there."

Samira looked at him and saw tears in the dust on his face. She had no tears.

"He must be dead," she said.

"Yes," said Benyamin. There was no more to say.

But suddenly Samira knew there was something else to say.

"I'm glad you didn't die, Benyamin," she said. "There are two of us here."

Then she did cry.

Celia Barker Lottridge

TWO

The Orphan Section

Baqubah Refugee Camp
September 1918

MAYBE HAMADAN was a city, but all Samira could see were brown tents and brown late-summer fields. The British army was camped far outside the city walls. She stayed under the chinar trees with hundreds of other ragged people and ate stew and bread brought by British soldiers. She was given a quilt to wrap around her at night.

It was peaceful there beside the British army. But after two days the journey began again. This time the people rode in big wagons for a week until they came to a place where there were more tents — big white ones.

This was the Baqubah Refugee Camp near Baghdad, where they would stay until the war was over and they could go home.

Before they could enter the camp, all the refugees had to go through water that would kill lice and other things that might cause sickness. The water was in a big tank. It was cool and so deep that it came up to Samira's chin. She washed herself from her hair to her feet with strong yellow soap.

When she came out a woman handed her a towel and checked her hair to be sure no lice were left.

"My clothes?" asked Samira, clutching the towel around her.

Celia Barker Lottridge

"Oh, they're gone," said the woman. "Burned. Go into the next tent and you'll get new ones."

Samira was given a long skirt, a loose blouse that hung over it and a shawl. The skirt and blouse were too big and the fabric was rough, but Samira liked the color, a blue that reminded her of Mama's favorite scarf. And everything was clean.

The girls and women were sent to tents on one side of the camp and the men and boys to the other side. Samira looked anxiously for Benyamin but she couldn't see him anywhere.

"Will I be able to see my brother?" she asked a man in a uniform. He was trying to hurry everyone along and barely glanced at her.

"We have to try to find your parents," he said briskly. "For now you are assigned to this tent." He gave her a little push toward one of the tents and turned away.

The tent was crowded with women and children. There were women alone and others with their daughters and small sons. There were some girls who were alone, too, but Samira didn't want to talk to any of them. They were all strangers and they looked at her with questions in their eyes. She found that if she sat very still no one noticed her most of the time.

There was a stove in a shelter outside the tent. Every day the soldiers brought food to be warmed. Sacks of bread and kettles of soup made of beans or lentils. As Samira ate monotonous soup from her tin cup she tried not to remember her mother's stews, seasoned with herbs and vegetables picked from the garden.

After a meal each person took her cup to a washing-up place. One day as Samira was swishing her cup through the basin of soapy water, she caught sight of Benyamin walking past. She dropped the cup and called to him.

"Benyamin, I'm here!"

"Little sister," he said, coming to her quickly. "I'm glad you saw me. No one could tell me which tent you were in. Now I've heard that they'll be moving everyone to different parts of the camp. We must tell them that we want to be in the same section. Will you remember?"

Samira was indignant. "Of course I'll remember. We have to be together. There are so many tents here and more people than in Ayna. Maybe more than in the city! We have to be together or we will never see each other!"

"Good. I think they'll listen to us." Benyamin touched her hand and was gone.

The next day a man with a large flat book and a pen came into the tent. He went from one person to another, asking questions and writing words in the book. When Samira's turn came she told him about her parents and Maryam.

"They died on the journey," she said. "But my brother is here. Benyamin. He's in one of the tents for the men. I know there are tents for families. Send us to one of those so that we can be together. Please."

The man smiled. "There are so many kinds of people in this camp," he said. "Armenians, Assyrians from the mountains and Assyrians like you from the plains near Urmieh. Some are parents with their children and others are men or women or children who are here without their families. Each group will have a section of the camp. You and your

Celia Barker Lottridge

brother will be in a section for Assyrian orphans. You will be able to see your brother, I promise. Now I must go and talk with someone else."

Samira knew the word orphan. There was a boy in the village whose parents had died of an illness. He was an orphan, people said, but he went to live with his uncle's family. He didn't go to a special place.

She wondered about this place. A place for children with no parents.

The next day a woman came to Samira's tent. She called together all the girls who were there without a mother.

"Today everyone is moving to the part of the camp where they will live. You are going to the Assyrian Orphan Section. Hold hands and follow me. You big girls, watch out that you don't let go of the small ones. I don't want anyone to get lost."

She led them out of the tent. They made a long line, like a snake. The snake of girls wound its way through crowds of people who were talking and calling to each other as they moved along. They went down a long row of big white tents, around a corner and down another row.

The girl behind Samira squeezed her hand and spoke in her ear.

"So many tents," she said. "So many people! Do you think there are any people left in Persia?"

Samira shrugged.

The girl squeezed her hand again.

"I'm Anna," she said. "I know what's going to happen. They are going to give me some little children to look after. That's all right but I want to do it with someone like you. I think you have good sense."

Samira almost laughed. "Good sense?"

"You're quiet. You don't fuss. Shall we stick together?"

Samira turned to look at the girl behind her. Anna had noticed her as she sat on her sleeping mat, but she hadn't noticed Anna at all. Now she saw a girl with a round face and big eyes smiling at her.

Samira smiled back. It felt strange, as if her mouth had forgotten how to turn up at the corners.

"Yes," said Samira. "We'll stick together."

At last the snake of children came to a wire fence with a gate in it. The woman opened the gate and the line followed her through. Then they all dropped hands and looked at a big open space with tents on either side.

The woman said, "You girls and the littlest boys will be in the tents over there. The boys' tents are on the other side."

"Good," said Samira to herself. Benyamin would not be far away.

"There's an eating tent down at the end," the woman went on, "and a school tent. Right here we'll build a playground where you can swing and climb."

Samira understood everything but the playground. Why would anyone need a special place to play? But the school tent sounded promising. Maybe at last she could go to school.

The woman was busy sorting the girls into tents.

"I want a few of you older girls in each tent. You'll help look after the little ones." She looked at Anna. "I'm sure you'll be good at that." Then she noticed Samira. "And you can help, too, dear," she added kindly.

Samira almost laughed again.

"How did you know that would happen?" she asked Anna.

"It always happens," said Anna. "I'm only ten but I guess I'm tall for my age. Maybe she can see that I've looked after my little sisters." She stopped and looked away, as if she wished she hadn't spoken about her sisters.

"I looked after my sister, Maryam," said Samira quickly. "She loved songs. But she's not with me because—"

"You'll tell me about her when we have time. Right now we have to find our spot in this tent."

Anna went over to the piles of sleeping mats and quilts that had been left at the door.

Samira stood still, feeling puzzled. It seemed that Anna didn't want to hear about Maryam. Or maybe she didn't want to talk about her own sisters.

She took a deep breath and went to help Anna choose a spot at the far end of the tent where they wouldn't be crowded on both sides. They laid out their mats and put the quilts and their small bundles of clothes neatly against the canvas wall.

When time came for the midday meal, Samira was pleased to find that the boys and girls ate at the same time. Every day she could speak with her brother.

It was strange. At home with the whole family together in their little house there were days and days when she and Benyamin hardly talked to each other. They lived separate lives. Here in the camp each of them wanted to be sure that the other was really there, that they were still together, so they talked often.

Most days Benyamin went out into the camp with other boys to collect laundry or deliver food supplies, and he brought back news and stories. One afternoon at the beginning of winter he came with big news.

"The war is over," he said. "Turkey and Britain are no longer fighting."

"No war," said Samira. She could hardly believe it. "So we'll go home soon!"

Benyamin shook his head. "They say it will be a long time before everything gets back to the way it was. We have to stay here for a while."

"How long?" asked Samira.

But Benyamin didn't know, and Samira didn't get a chance to ask anyone else.

The girls never had a reason to leave the Orphan Section. Each morning Samira and Anna folded their nightgowns, put them away in the boxes they had been given, rolled up their sleeping mats with the quilts inside and lined everything up along the wall. Then they helped the little children dress and tidy away their beds. They took a turn at sweeping the canvas floor with the broom that was kept by the doorway. That took care of housework.

Stacks of clothes that needed mending arrived at the tent door, and the girls spent most mornings sewing on buttons and patching worn shirts and blouses. In the afternoon they took the smaller children outside and played games with them and told them stories.

For a while it was fun to try out the strange structures that had been put in the playground. They sat at either end of a long plank and tipped up and down, or perched on a wooden seat hung from a metal frame and swung back and forth. Sometimes boys too old to be in the orphan tents would sneak over the fence and swing too high or tip too hard. The boards broke. No one fixed them. The girls could only look at the useless playground and shake their heads.

The one day that was different was Sunday, when a priest or a missionary came to the Orphan Section and led a church service. Sometimes the Bible stories were interesting but, as Anna said, church services did not exactly add excitement to their lives.

Weeks passed. It grew cold at night and the orphans were given extra quilts. Then it started to rain. The tents leaked at the seams and there was no way to keep everything dry. Some nights Samira could hardly sleep for all the coughing. Nurses came to check for signs of real illness and sometimes a child was taken to the hospital tent, but Samira and Anna and Benyamin stayed well.

"I guess the people who run this camp can say they are keeping us safe here," said Anna. "But we might go crazy because nothing happens. How long can this go on?"

Samira just shrugged. Winter had almost passed. It seemed that it could go on for a very long time.

ONE SPRING morning a woman came to the Orphan Section carrying a heavy canvas bag. She gathered all the girls who were at least seven years old and led them to the unused school tent. She sat on a rug in the middle of the tent. The girls watched her carefully and sat down around her.

The woman reached into the bag and took out a book. She opened it and held it so that all the girls could see the page. Samira saw that it had writing like the writing in the big books in the church in Ayna. It also had a picture of a fox standing in a vineyard.

The woman began to read words from the book. They made a story, a little story about a fox who wanted to eat a bunch of grapes.

When the story was finished, the woman said, "Would you girls like to be able to read such a story?"

Samira answered at once. "Yes. Yes, I want to read. Will you teach us?"

"I will," said the woman. "That's why I'm here. Have any of you been to school?"

Two of the bigger girls nodded. One had gone to her village school, the only girl among all the boys.

"My parents wanted me to be able to read," she said. "The teacher gave me a place to sit right by his desk. It was hard with all those boys staring at my back."

The other girl, Naomi, had gone to the girls' school run by the mission in the city.

"My uncle went to work in America," she said. "When he came back he told my mother that girls there study just the way boys do. She decided that I should have a chance to be educated. So I lived at the school and learned. But then the war came."

Everyone knew what had happened then. After all, here Naomi was, with the other orphans.

The teacher said, "You two girls can read stories to the little ones and help them learn their letters. You will be assistant teachers."

Samira hardly heard. She was remembering how her

mother had spoken to the priest in Ayna about getting a teacher for the girls. Now she had a teacher. Now she could learn to read.

Not every girl was so enthusiastic. Some found that trying to make sense of the markings in the books made them tired. They were glad when each day's lesson was over. But Samira loved it. Once she understood that each mark should make a sound in her head, the words seemed to jump off the paper into her mind.

But the teacher only had a few books, and it was not many weeks before Samira was reading them for the second time.

"You can help me," said the teacher. "I have no way to get more books in Syriac so I want you to write something for the little girls to read. Something they can understand. I have colored pencils. Maybe someone will draw pictures."

Samira said she would try, but lying in bed that night she thought, "I don't know what to write. There's nothing here that makes me think of a story."

She said to the teacher, "I can write letters and words but a book is not just letters and words. What can I write about?"

"Before you came here you lived in your village," said the teacher. "Write about something you remember." She looked at Samira's face. "Something happy, before the bad things happened. It's good to remember something happy."

For many days Samira couldn't write any words about her village. She practiced the letters and wrote her name over and over until it looked perfect. But every story she could think of ended up with everybody running away, and she didn't want to write about that.

Then one suppertime the rice and vegetable stew had a new warm and spicy taste. Some of the little girls made faces, but Samira sat with her spoon in her hand, remembering.

It was the taste of peppers, small red ones that her mother dried and put in stews. Just a little because, as she said to Samira, "These are hot hot hot! If you eat one by itself it will burn your mouth! Remember, a small pepper goes a long way."

Samira sat in the eating tent with that taste in her mouth. She could hear Mama's voice in her head and she almost cried, but she remembered something else, too. Something that could be a story for the little girls.

It was hard work writing a story. Samira had to write it over and over before she was satisfied. It needed pictures, too, but she had a plan about the pictures. She had noticed that Anna drew curling vines and flowers, donkeys and sheep instead of practicing her letters.

One day after a long writing lesson she told Samira, "When we go home I'll get married and have a house and a garden and some children. I won't write."

"I don't know what will happen when I go home," said Samira. "But I've written a story about something that happened when I was small. I know you can draw the right pictures for my story. Will you do it?"

"I'll try," said Anna. "What's the story about?"

"Listen," said Samira.

Zena was a little girl who lived in a house that looked like this.

The story told about how Zena and her family slept on the roof in hot weather and how Zena and her friends played on the roof. And Zena's mother spread fruit and vegetables on the roof to dry in the sun.

Anna drew a picture of a little house with a flat roof and a ladder that went up to the roof.

Zena's mother said, "These fruits and vegetables are for winter. Do not touch them. Do not eat them." Zena always obeyed her mother, but one day she was playing with her friend on the roof and they saw berries drying there. Delicious red berries, and only half dry so they would be juicy.

Zena could not help it. She ran over and picked up one bright berry and popped it in her mouth.

But it was not a berry. It was a tiny hot pepper. Very very hot in Zena's mouth. It made her cry. It made her face turn red. It hurt her mouth.

She could not tell her mother. Never. But her mother knew. She looked at Zena's red face and her teary eyes. She shook her head.

"You disobeyed me," she said. "You will see. In the winter we need every piece of fruit and every pepper." Then she smiled. "But I will not punish you. The pepper has done that. You will always remember." Zena nodded and she never did forget.

Anna finished the pictures. Looking at them Samira knew that Anna's village was just like hers.

She thought of Maryam and said softly, "Your sisters would like these pictures."

Anna nodded but she didn't say anything.

Samira stitched the pages together to make a book. The girls in the class loved to read it. Many of them could remember sleeping up on the roofs with their families. They grew quiet, remembering, but they laughed when Zena bit into the hot pepper.

"Will you write a book for the boys, too?" asked Benyamin. "One about playing games in the street or banging on pans to keep the foxes from eating the grapes."

"You have to tell me about it," said Samira. "I never did any of those things."

After supper that evening Benyamin sat with Samira and told her how it was to stay in the vineyard watchtower all night, on the lookout for foxes.

"When there was no moon it was very dark," he said. "If foxes got in and ate the grapes, our fathers beat us so we wouldn't let it happen again."

"How terrible," said Samira.

"Not so terrible," said Benyamin. "Just a little, so we would be more careful. And our father?" He stopped for a minute. "Once he crept into the vineyard just to test us. We heard him and thought it was a wolf, it sounded so big. We were afraid to come out so we threw down the iron pot that was empty after dinner and hit him, but not where it hurt too much." He smiled, remembering. "Papa just laughed and said we were good watchmen."

That story made a good book for the little boys. Anna had trouble drawing the foxes, and Benyamin said they looked too much like dogs. But the boys didn't care. They wanted to read the story again and again.

Samira always collected both books each time they were used and put them carefully in the bottom of her clothes box. It felt as if she had saved a piece of Ayna on those pages, and she wanted to keep them safe.

The teacher liked the stories, too.

"They remind me of villages I've visited," she said. "I

Celia Barker Lottridge

remember the fruit, how delicious it is. And I remember seeing children looking at me over the walls at the edges of the roofs."

"Not anymore," said Samira. "There is no one to look after the houses. Every year my father put more clay on the roof. Every year he whitewashed the walls. Now our house will crumble away."

"The war is over but it takes time for things to settle down," said the teacher. "Little by little people will return."

"When I came here I was nine," said Samira. "Now I've been here more than a year so I must be ten. How old will I be when I can go home?"

But the teacher didn't know.

FALL AND WINTER passed. Then another summer was nearly over. Samira knew that she must be eleven years old. She could read any book the teacher could find and was using a slate to work on adding and subtracting, but in the Orphan Section life did not change.

Then one day after class the teacher said to Samira and Anna, "Stay here for a minute, please. Nurse MacDonald is coming to talk with you. She's in charge of the babies who are too young to be in the Orphan Section."

"Maybe she wants us to leave the Orphan Section and work in the nursery," Anna whispered to Samira.

"What if she only wants you?" asked Samira. "You're the one who is good with babies."

But there was no time to talk. A small woman in a nurse's uniform was greeting them.

"I've heard that you two girls are very good with the little children," she said.

Anna looked quickly at Samira and raised her eyebrows. Then she said, "We both looked after children before we came to this place. Do you want to give us a job?"

"Not a job," said Nurse MacDonald. "A little boy. He was a tiny baby when he came here with his mother soon after the camp opened. She was so weak from the journey that she died before she could tell us her name or his. We named him Elias. He's strong and healthy and now he's nearly two. We thought he could come to your tent and be a kind of little brother to you two girls."

Samira thought of Maryam. "A little brother would be a big responsibility." She stepped closer to Anna. "The three of us would have to stay together. Like a family. They couldn't send one of us away from the others."

The nurse looked surprised. "We don't send people away."

"But you could," said Anna. "We're orphans. There's no one to say a word if you decide I'm old enough to live with the women and work in the nursery and never see Samira. Or Elias." She was quiet for a long moment. Samira wondered what she was thinking.

Finally Anna said, "Samira and I know what it's like to have little sisters. We want to keep this little brother with us. Not lose him. So you must write down that Anna and Samira and Elias will stay together. And it must be signed by a British officer."

"I'm an officer in the medical corps," said Nurse Macdonald. "If it will make you feel better I'll write you a letter. It will be in English, of course."

She took paper from her bag and began to write. As she

Celia Barker Lottridge

wrote she smiled, and Samira knew that she was thinking, "What will these girls ever do with this letter? I might as well give it to them."

Samira moved close to Anna.

"What good is this paper to us? We can't read it and we have nowhere to keep it."

"I've seen how the British want everything written down. The paper might help if they ever wanted to separate us. I'll put it in the bottom of my clothes box and keep it safe."

Elias arrived with Nurse MacDonald the next afternoon. He had curly black hair and round dark eyes. He walked into the tent and looked quickly from Anna to Samira and then all around his new home. When he saw that there was plenty of space for running, he ran. Samira darted to the door so he wouldn't go outside, and Anna managed to keep him from racing through a group of girls who were sitting on the floor sewing. He was very fast.

When he finally stopped, Anna picked him up and said, "Elias, I'm Anna, your new sister, and this is Samira, your other sister. You're going to live here with us."

Elias cocked his head as if he liked the sound of her voice. Then he wiggled to show that he wanted to get down. This time he walked from one end of the tent to the other, looking at everything. Then he began to run again.

Nurse MacDonald quickly said goodbye. When she was gone, Anna and Samira looked at each other and laughed. They could see why she needed to get this boy out of the nursery.

"He'll be a full-time responsibility for a while," Anna said.

Samira nodded. "For once I'm glad there's a fence around the Orphan Section. At least we can't lose him completely."

By suppertime Elias was tired of running. He came straight to Samira and leaned against her.

"He needs something to eat before he falls asleep," said Anna. She got some bread and milk from the eating tent, and Elias ate it with his eyes nearly closed.

"I don't think he'll have any trouble sleeping tonight," said Samira, and she laid him on his sleeping mat between her mat and Anna's and covered him up.

When she woke the next morning she was relieved to see that the little boy was still there. He opened his eyes and looked at her for a long time. Then he turned his head and looked at Anna. And then he sat up, ready to start running.

"I think he's made up his mind," said Samira. "He's willing to stay with us."

Helping Elias settle in kept Samira and Anna very busy for several days. He didn't talk much but he had a way of deciding what he wanted to do and simply setting out to do it. The girls had to keep up with him or he would try to climb the tent poles or unroll all the sleeping mats. To keep him busy they marched around the outdoor area counting and singing songs with him. They all slept very well at night.

But as another winter began, Elias settled into a routine, just like everyone else in the Orphan Section. He even learned to let Samira and Anna do their lessons in the school tent and the chilly days went by, one very much like the others.

ONE MORNING Samira opened her eyes and noticed that the light was brighter and the air had a warm feel to it.

"I think it's spring," she said to Anna.

Still, she was surprised when the woman who came to check the height and weight of all the children in the Orphan Section said, "You'll be turning twelve one of these days. When you came here in summer of 1918 you had turned nine in the spring. Now it's the spring of 1921. Do you know exactly when your birthday is?"

"I don't know the day but it's at the time when the storks come back to their nests in the tower of the church," said Samira. She suddenly remembered the big long-necked birds sitting on their untidy nests waiting for their eggs to hatch, and Mama laughing at how funny they looked.

"The storks," said Samira. "I want to see them again."

But the woman had gone on to measure another girl and didn't hear her. Samira caught up with her as she was leaving the tent.

"If I'm twelve that means I have been here for three years," she said. "Will I be here forever?"

"Of course not," said the woman. "The camp won't be here forever. It will close one of these days."

"But if the camp isn't here where will we go?" Samira thought of the storks again. "Home. We should go home."

"I know," said the woman. She looked sad. "It is not always easy to go home after a war. Things have changed. I'm sorry. I don't know what will happen."

Samira began to listen carefully to the talk around her. But she only heard questions. "When…?" "Where…?" "How long…?"

Rumors spread through the camp. Benyamin and his friend Ashur reported a new one every day when they came in from delivering laundry. Samira began to get a picture of what was going to happen.

The camp would soon be closed but the people in the camp would not be allowed to return to the villages they had left behind in Persia. Instead they would be sent to villages up north, in country that had been part of Turkey before the war. And boys just a little older than Benyamin would go into an army to defend those villages.

No one knew what would happen to the orphans.

"What can we say if they just send us somewhere?" asked Samira.

"Well, I won't go without you and Elias," said Anna.

Elias came and stood between the two girls. He had been with them nearly a year and now he wanted to talk as much as he had wanted to run when they first knew him.

He looked up and said, "Where? Going where?"

"We don't know where we'll go but we'll all go together," Samira said, picking him up. He was heavy now but she could still give him a squeeze before she put him down.

The very next day a man came into the tent before breakfast. They had never seen him before. He waited until all the children noticed him and became quiet. Then he spoke.

"This camp will be closing soon, and everyone in it will have to go and live somewhere else. The Assyrian men and women who are in the camp have been offered the chance to settle in villages not far from here. They have refused this offer because they want to return to the villages they came from. They will have to find their own way back. It will be hard but they have chosen. You are children and you can't find your own way so you'll be sent to another orphanage. You don't have to worry. You will be looked after."

Samira stared at the man. How could he tell her not to worry?

The man must have felt the questions in the eyes of all the children because he said, "That's all I can tell you now. I'm sorry." He turned and left the tent.

Samira turned to Anna. "First our villages are gone. Now the camp will be gone. We have been here for almost three years of our lives. Where will we go next?"

Life in the camp changed quickly. One after another the big tents outside the Orphan Section were taken down. The teacher stopped coming to the school tent. Garbage piled up as group after group of men, women and families were sent away.

"They have to walk all the way to Mosul," said Benyamin. "There they have to sign a paper saying that they are leaving the camp because they want to. Then they'll camp somewhere along the Tigris River until they can cross over and walk to Persia and, maybe, back to their villages."

There was nothing for the orphans to do but wait. The girls still swept the tent every day, but the laundry was closed so the children's clothes got dirtier and dirtier. Benyamin's shirt was torn and there was no thread to mend it. Bean soup and bread arrived every day but the bread was not fresh. The bakers had gone.

When at last news came that the orphans should prepare to leave for Baghdad, Samira was relieved. The Baqubah refugee camp was not a place to be anymore.

She made a bundle of her extra blouse and skirt and the

books she had stitched together. Elias's clothes made a smaller bundle. Anna unraveled some thread from a worn-out blanket and sewed a special pocket into her skirt for the paper about Elias. Then she bundled her things. They were ready to go.

Everyone stood in the hot sun while the soldiers took the big tents down. Six tents where one hundred and fifty children had lived. The older boys were put to work loading the cooking pots and other equipment into big canvas bags.

When everything was packed, the soldiers led them through the orphans' gate, past the dusty squares where hundreds of tents had stood, and out of the camp.

Outside the gates were two big wagons and oxen to pull them. The soldiers and the older boys loaded the tents and the canvas bags into the wagons. Samira could see that the wagons were getting filled up.

"There's no room for us," she said to Anna.

"You'll have to walk," said one of the soldiers. "We've been ordered to take all this equipment, and it certainly can't walk."

Benyamin came over. "If the small children have to walk it will be a very slow trip and hard for them, too."

The soldier looked at the crowd of children.

"They only gave us these two wagons," he said.

"I have an idea," said Samira. "The boys can make a place on top of the tents where the little ones can ride. The rest of us can walk."

"Go ahead," said the soldier, and he watched while Benyamin and Ashur and other big boys climbed to the top of the wagons. They jumped and punched to make nests in the canvas. Then they lifted the small children up into the nests and said, "Now you must sit still or you'll fall out and have to walk."

Samira could see the children peering down. Elias waved to her.

"We'll be right behind you," she called.

It was hard for the children who were walking to keep up with the wagons. The road was hot under their bare feet, and the sun beat down. Sometimes the wagons stopped and they rested for a few minutes. The soldiers gave them water and dried fruit, but they were soon back on the road.

The journey took two days. At night they slept beside the road on bedrolls. The soldiers kept watch, and Samira wondered what they were watching for.

In the middle of the night she woke up, looking for someone. Mama. Where was Mama?

Samira stared at the darkness. No. This was a different walk. Three years had passed. Mama was gone.

She put her hand on the lump that was Elias under his blanket and waited until the soldier came by, dark against the stars. Then she could sleep again.

The second day they started out before the sun had risen.

"It's going to be a hot day," one of the soldiers explained. "We want to get to Baghdad before the sun is high."

Before noon they came to an army encampment near the river on the edge of the city.

"This is as far as we go," said the soldiers. They lifted the small children down from the wagons. "Someone from the orphanage will come to get you. They'll take you into the city by truck. Wait here under these trees." And they went away.

The trees offered only scattered shade, and Samira was worrying that the sun might burn them to cinders when several army trucks arrived and a big woman with brown hair that curled all over her head climbed out of one of them. Her blue eyes reminded Samira of the teacher in the Baqubah camp.

"I'm Mrs. McDowell," she said. "I've come to take you to the orphanage in Baghdad but I hope you won't be staying long." She smiled. "We want to get you back to Persia soon."

Persia. The word rippled through the crowd of children and then the word "home" and the word "villages."

Mrs. McDowell shook her head.

"My dears," she said. "We can only go one step at a time. That step is Baghdad. The next step is Persia. After that, we can only hope and pray. Now come. Get yourselves into the trucks."

As she struggled to keep her balance in the bouncing truck, Samira thought of those words. Baghdad was the next step. Maybe the first step on the journey home.

Later, Samira could only remember three things about Baghdad. One was the heat. It was so hot that it was impossible to walk out of the orphanage building in bare feet. The very earth felt as hot as an iron pot over a fire.

Another was clothes. Mrs. McDowell was horrified at the shabby clothes the children were wearing. She brought some refugee women to teach the oldest girls to make shirts and trousers for the boys and dresses for the girls.

The dresses were all made of green cloth with little yellow flowers. Samira looked at Anna and thought, "That is what I look like. How strange."

Mrs. McDowell seemed to read her mind. "I wish we had more colors, but we're lucky to get enough cloth to cover you all."

Samira was glad to have a dress that was bright and the right size, but she was even happier with her new shoes. They had thick rubber soles and soft tops that tied around her ankles. In those shoes she could walk on burning hot tile or stony roads. She could go anywhere.

But the orphans were not going anywhere.

They were waiting. That was the third thing Samira remembered about Baghdad. Everyone was waiting. She saw crowds of people by the river, camped out and waiting to be allowed to cross over and walk to Persia. She saw men and women waiting in long lines to get passage to India or America. She heard people talking about where they could go if they had permission, if they had money, if they could make contact with their relatives.

Mrs. McDowell said, "It's the war. So many people had to leave their homes. Now they need to find somewhere in this world where they can be safe and happy."

Then, suddenly, the orphans weren't waiting anymore. Mrs. McDowell came to the schoolroom right in the middle of a lesson, waving a paper.

"Children," she said. "This says that the Assyrian orphans, all of you, can cross the border. You won't be going to your own villages but you will be in Persia, near the city of Kermanshah. Oh, my dear children. It's the next step."

They went by train. It was exciting and frightening, climbing up the high iron steps into a narrow space with rows of seats covered with scratchy cloth. The strangeness made some of the little ones cry. Elias didn't cry but his eyes were wide with wonder and fear. Comforting him made Samira and Anna brave. They didn't really notice the jerk and rattle of the train as it moved out of the station. They were busy talking to Elias.

"Look," said Samira. "Look at all those people waving goodbye. They think we are very lucky to be on this train. Only us. Only the orphans can go now. Everyone else has to wait."

Mrs. McDowell sat down in the seat facing the children. She was fanning herself with her handkerchief.

"It's been such a rush," she said. "When we heard that we could take you to Kermanshah we had to move quickly. You never know when the permit might be revoked."

"Revoked?" said Samira. "What does that mean?"

"It would mean they changed their minds," said Mrs. McDowell. "These government officials seem to do nothing but change their minds. They let some of the Assyrians across the border weeks ago and then made them come back."

"What about us? Will they make us come back?"

"No," said Mrs. McDowell. "They know you orphans will stay where they put you. But they also know that some of the Assyrians will do almost anything to try to get back to their villages. The only way to stop them is to keep them on this side of the border."

"Why do they want to stop them?" said Anna. "All of us should go back to the places we came from, to our homes."

"There is still fighting going on." Mrs. McDowell shook her head. "And travel is very dangerous. For the moment you children will be in the camp we're making at Kermanshah." She looked out the window at the dusty land and added, "At least I can promise you that Kermanshah will be cooler than Baghdad."

It was true. When they arrived in Kermanshah the air was clear and cool. The children stood on the train platform, breathing in fresh air and staring up at high mountains.

"It feels a little bit like home," said Samira. "What mountains are those?"

"The Zagros Mountains," said Mrs. McDowell. "Your village is beyond those mountains. A long distance beyond. Impossible to reach right now."

"But Kermanshah is another step," said Samira.

"Yes, it is," said Mrs. McDowell. "Where I come from we would say it's a step in the right direction."

SAMIRA AND ANNA stood at the door of their tent and looked around. The Kermanshah camp stood on the edge of a lake in beautiful open fields with the mountains beyond. The tents were exactly like the ones at Baqubah. There were seven of them — six for sleeping and a big one for eating.

"I think this is the same tent we were in before," said Samira. "I recognize that place where it's mended."

Later she said to Benyamin, "If I sleep in a tent for three years, is that tent my home?"

"Of course not. We live in these tents because we have to. Some day we'll get home. Home to Ayna."

"How can we?" asked Samira. "They tell us over and over that it's impossible."

"We have to find a way," said Benyamin. "I'm afraid they'll put me and the other boys in the army when we're sixteen. I won't go into any army, so I have to get back to Ayna."

"You won't be sixteen very soon, will you?" asked Samira, wondering how it could be that she wasn't sure how old her own brother was.

"I turned fifteen in Baghdad," said Benyamin. "So I have another year to be an orphan."

"I'm twelve," said Samira. "I can be an orphan for a few more years."

She looked past Benyamin and saw seven tents and an empty field — places to sleep and eat and play. Nothing that was hers.

"I have to get back to Ayna, too," she said in a low voice. Then, louder, "When I'm too old to be an orphan I have nowhere to go, not even the army."

"You could get married. Lots of girls get married when they're fifteen or sixteen."

"You think I could get married here? In one of these tents? Without a village to live in? No!"

Samira suddenly realized that she was shouting at Benyamin as if he could change something.

Just then they heard the sharp sound of a mallet hitting a board three times. It was the signal that the orphans should gather in the big open area beside the cluster of tents.

Benyamin gave Samira a half smile.

"Good news?" he said. But he shook his head and they walked together to join the others.

A tall man with a beard stood in front of one hundred and fifty children.

Celia Barker Lottridge

"I have some things to tell you," he said, "and I hope you can understand me. I've only been studying Syriac for a short time and I know I make mistakes. As you know Mrs. McDowell has returned to Baghdad. My name is Mr. Edwards. I'm with the Near East Relief in the city of Hamadan, and we run this orphanage. You'll be living here for several months until we can move you into proper buildings in Hamadan."

Samira could feel the children around her sigh and slump, but Mr. Edwards was going on.

"You'll be sleeping in these tents and we'll build a kitchen and a schoolroom that will double as an eating hall. School will start as soon as we can bring in a teacher or two. You'll have jobs to do but you can have fun, too. You are in no danger here. You can run in the field and swim in the lake. You may not be where you want to be, but you are in Persia. Welcome!"

Mr. Edwards was kind, and Samira could see that he worked hard, but he often had to be away in Hamadan. The cook stayed but the teachers, nurses and other helpers came for a few weeks and then went off to other more permanent orphanages.

"We should be able to leave and go somewhere else the way these other people do," Anna grumbled. "But, no, we have to stay here where there's nothing to do but odd jobs."

The boys helped the builders and the girls took turns in the kitchen. When there was a teacher they went to school. Otherwise the children found ways to entertain themselves. As long as the summer lasted they went swimming in the lake. The boys played games with sticks out in the fields and the girls kept the young ones busy on the lakeshore.

Then the autumn rains came, and the tents leaked just as they had in Baqubah. One morning the grass sparkled with frost. Samira rooted through the ragbag of worn-out clothes to find a jacket she could mend for Elias. More jackets and quilts arrived, but they never seemed quite warm enough in the sharp mountain air.

Every morning when Samira came out of the tent she looked at the mountains. The Zagros Mountains. Mama and Maryam lay in the earth somewhere in those mountains, and Papa, too. But on the other side was home.

Benyamin came and stood beside her one day.

"I'm off to gather fuel for the kitchen," he said. "There's always some job to do. But nothing that matters." He stared at the mountains, frowning. "The builders say that some people have made the journey, that they are back in their villages." He looked at Samira and she could see the longing in his eyes.

"Don't listen," she said sharply. "It's only talk."

"It's not only talk," said Benyamin. "Some people have made it."

He turned and walked away.

Samira's heart was heavy. She wanted to get over those mountains, too, but she was afraid. For Elias and the other little children, she told herself. But really she knew. She remembered the journey through the mountains too well. It was for herself that she was afraid.

One morning when it was barely light, Samira heard someone calling her name from the doorway of the tent. She crawled out from under her quilt, wrapped it around her and stepped out into the cold air.

Ashur stood there looking at her, not saying anything.

"Why are you here? Where's Benyamin?"

"He's gone," Ashur said at last. "So are Yakob and Simon. I think they've gone away to the mountains. They're going to try to get home."

Samira didn't want to make sense out of the words he was saying.

"Benyamin's gone? Are you sure?"

"I'm sure. He sleeps beside me and he's not there. He's taken his warm clothes and his knife. Yakob and Simon are gone, too. I woke everyone in the tent. We realize now that each one of them had been talking about getting over the mountains and going home. I guess they just couldn't wait anymore."

He stopped talking as Elias came through the tent door and leaned against Samira. He had put on his trousers and his thick shirt, but his feet were bare.

"Why are you out here?" he asked Samira. "It's cold."

"I'll come in and get dressed," said Samira automatically and followed Elias into the tent.

When Anna saw them she said sharply, "Where have you two been? Something has happened, hasn't it?"

"Benyamin's gone. He's gone, Anna. He went with Yakob and Simon to go through the mountains and get home."

"Benyamin? He's run away from the camp? Benyamin? Are you sure?"

"Ashur is sure. Benyamin said nothing to me. And he went without me."

"He wouldn't have taken you into the mountains," said Anna. "And if he had told you, you would have found a way to stop him."

Elias looked up at Samira. "He told me," he said solemnly.

"What did he tell you?"

"He told me he had to go away but I would see him again and I should stay near you so you wouldn't be too lonely."

Suddenly Samira was angry. "He was afraid to tell me. He did what he wanted and now I have to sit here and worry. Maybe I'll never see him again."

She looked down at Elias. He looked ready to cry. She knelt down and hugged him.

"You didn't do anything wrong," she said. "It was Benyamin who did a foolish thing."

She looked around. All the girls in the tent were sitting up and staring at her.

"I have to talk to Mr. Edwards," she said to Anna. "Right now."

She found Mr. Edwards in the school building. He came to her and took her hands for a moment.

"I've heard about Benyamin," he said. "I know how worried you must be. I thought Benyamin had more sense. He knows how rough those mountains are. Very cold, too, so early in the spring."

"Can't someone go and look for them?"

"I won't send any of the other boys into the mountains and there is no one else to go. We'll get messages out so that people in the villages and the men working on the roads will be on the lookout. The boys will have to seek help sometime. All we can do here is pray. I'm sorry, Samira."

Samira went down to the lake. The morning sun was glinting on the water but the air was still cold. She pulled her jacket tight around her and wondered whether

Celia Barker Lottridge

Benyamin was cold. He had his warm jacket. But had he taken a quilt to wrap around him when he slept?

She looked at the mountains beyond the lake. They looked like a solid wall. The very idea of walking into those mountains made her shiver. But that's what Benyamin was doing.

She heard footsteps and turned to see Elias bringing her a folded piece of lawash. He handed it to her without a word and to please him she ate it. The bread was spread with honey, and its sweetness and familiar taste were comforting.

"Thank you, Elias," she said. "I don't want to go to school today. Shall I come and read stories to you and your friends?"

"Yes," said Elias. "Read us your books."

As Samira read the stories she had written long ago about Ayna, she thought that the village Benyamin might return to would not be like the village she remembered. No one to welcome him. The gardens in ruins. The houses falling in. That's what he would find.

At supper Mr. Edwards told them that no word had been heard about the boys.

"But they haven't been gone for even a day yet," he said. "I'm sure we'll get news before long. Remember that Benyamin and Yakob and Simon are strong boys and smart, too. I think they will find that they have made a mistake and be safe with us again." He looked around the room at the silent children. "I know you want to get home, too, but I'm sure you understand that this is not the way to do it."

As soon as it was dark Samira went to bed, exhausted from worry and anger and sadness. She fell asleep at once and dreamed that she was crossing a deep chasm on an end-less bridge made of sticks that broke under her feet. She woke and lay staring into the darkness, remembering how Benyamin had held her steady on a bridge long ago.

When the gray light told her that it was very early morning, she quietly got up and dressed.

She stepped out of the tent and saw a white mist rising from the lake. The mountains were hidden, and as she walked along the shore she felt as if she was the only person awake in the whole world. But perhaps Benyamin was awake. Where had he slept?

The mist was blowing off the lake in wisps. It surrounded Samira and she could hardly see where she was going.

"I'd better go back," she thought. "I don't want to walk into the lake."

As she turned, she ran into something very solid.

Not a tree. There were no trees by the lake and this was not hard, like a tree. She looked up and saw a face looking down at her through the mist.

She jumped back. Her voice was a squeak.

"Benyamin? Is it you?"

"What are you doing out here?" Benyamin almost shouted.

Samira found her voice. "I'm here because you ran away! I've been so worried and you expect me to just sleep as usual?"

"I decided to come back," said Benyamin. "I've been walking all night."

"You don't sound very happy about it," said Samira. He was damp from the mist and looked as if he was awake by willpower alone. She felt herself shaking with relief. Benyamin was back.

"I'm not happy about it," he said, "but this is where I must be now. Samira, we walked to the mountains yesterday. Just before it got dark we came to a narrow valley. Papa and I came to a valley like that when we ran from the soldiers. Just before we went in Papa looked back to where you and Mama were far behind us and said, 'We should have stayed together.' That's what came into my mind and I knew I had to come back. No one was chasing me but I couldn't go on without you. I had to come back. Papa would say that we should stay together."

"I'm glad you thought of Papa," said Samira. "But what about Simon and Yakob?"

"They wanted to go on. They said that they were with each other and that was enough for them. They were angry with me but I thought of Papa and I knew he was right."

Samira said, "If we stay together we'll get somewhere. Maybe home. But somewhere. Now come and have some tea. It's nearly breakfast time and the cook will have water boiling. You must be very hungry."

When Mr. Edwards saw Benyamin, he asked him a few questions and then sent him to the tent to sleep. By suppertime everybody knew he was back. He could hardly eat because they were all asking him questions, mostly about Yakob and Simon.

"They went on," said Benyamin. "That's all I know. I gave them all my food and my knife so they'd have a spare. That was all I could do."

There was no news of the boys that night or the next day.

A week passed, and talk died down but the thought of them was in everyone's mind.

Anna said, "We will never know what happened to those two. I think they will be lost in the mountains forever."

But Anna was wrong.

When Yakob and Simon had been gone for eleven days, Mr. Edwards called all the children together. Samira came into the building hardly able to breathe. She was sure that she was about to hear terrible news, but when she saw Mr. Edwards' face she began to hope.

"Our two runaways were very lucky," he said. "Simon fell into a crevasse and broke his leg. It was impossible for Yakob to get him up the steep wall of rock so he stayed with him. They ran out of food and they wouldn't have lasted much longer but some Kurdish hunters found them and took them to their village. The Kurds took care of the boys until they could get them to the camp of one of the road crews. So Simon and Yakob are safe. Yakob will come back here. Simon will be in the town of Kermanshah where there's a doctor who can try to set his leg. After so many days I don't know how that will go. But they are both alive. We can thank God for that."

Three days later Yakob returned to the camp. Mr. Edwards told the children not to bother him with questions. The result was that everyone fell strangely silent when Yakob was near. Then they realized that Yakob wanted to talk.

"Benyamin has probably told you how foolish we were," he said. "We didn't have enough food or equipment for sleeping and cooking. When Simon fell I thought we were going to die and then the Kurds came. When we saw them we were frightened." He looked around at his friends. "Remember how afraid we were of the Kurds?"

"Of course," said Benyamin. "They did many terrible things to our people."

"I thought they would kill us," said Yakob. "But they took us to their village and fed us and took care of us. We were lucky that they found us. So that's our story. Thanks to the Kurds we're alive, but we didn't get home."

"We have to find another way," said Benyamin.

Summer came. One hot day when the children were all waiting for permission to go into the lake, a lady named Miss Watson came from Baghdad. She was thin and neat. None of the children had seen her before.

Samira and Anna, who were sitting in the shade of the schoolroom, heard her say to Mr. Edwards, "Shouldn't these children be in school on a Wednesday morning?"

"We have no teachers at the moment, Miss Watson. You people in Baghdad should know this. We've been waiting for a new teacher for the girls and then the boys' teacher got sick two weeks ago and left."

Miss Watson said, "I wasn't aware of the situation but it doesn't matter. I bring very good news. Read this document and call the children in. I'll tell them about it."

"What can it be?" Samira whispered to Anna. "Could they possibly be taking us back to our villages?"

Anna looked up at the mountains.

"Of course not," she said. "You know what they always say. The roads are still bad from the war. Travel is dangerous. There is still fighting. No, that's not the good news." Still, she followed Samira into the school building to hear the important announcement.

"Children," Miss Watson said. "I have come to tell you that this camp will be closing immediately. You are all going to Hamadan to live in a permanent orphanage. The British army has turned over a group of buildings to the Near East Relief. You won't live in tents anymore." She paused and looked at the rows of children.

Samira whispered to Anna, "Does she want us to cheer?"

Miss Watson went on quickly, "Your job now is to get everything packed and ready for the trucks when they come in a few days."

It was easy to see that Miss Watson thought they should all be very happy and grateful, but Samira didn't know what she felt. She said to Benyamin after the meeting, "Will this be a step in the right direction? Are you happy to go to Hamadan?"

"Hamadan is closer to the places all of us came from," said Benyamin. "So I guess it's the right direction. But she said it would be a permanent orphanage. That means it will be there forever. I hope they remember that we don't want to stay there forever."

Still, Samira began to look forward to being somewhere that was not a camp.

Days passed and no trucks came. Miss Watson had to agree with the children that they couldn't pack in advance. The cooking pots and dishes had to be used at every meal, and each child had only one change of clothes. There was nothing to do but wait.

Then, at last, on a morning at the very end of August,

Miss Watson gathered all one hundred and fifty children on the playing field.

"A message has come from the city," she said. "The trucks will be here by noon. Pack your things now. Girls, you are in charge of the smaller children. Boys, it's your job to take down the tents."

Now that they were really leaving, the children were filled with energy. Maybe they would not be left in the Hamadan Orphanage and forgotten. Right now Samira almost believed it.

It took the girls no more than ten minutes to pack their belongings. Samira stuffed her extra dress — too short, of course — her underwear and her books into a cotton bag. She rolled up her sleeping mat and the quilt that had not kept her warm in the winter.

When she looked around, all the other girls were packed, too.

Elias sat on his sleeping mat watching her, and she realized that he wasn't sure what was happening.

"Where are we going?" he asked. "Will we go on the train again?"

Samira sat down beside him. "Do you remember the train?"

He nodded. "Very loud."

"Yes, it was," said Samira. "Well, this time we'll go in trucks like the ones they bring supplies in. We get to ride in the back. It'll be fun. Lots of bouncing." She wasn't sure it would be fun, but it would be better than walking.

"But where are we going?"

"We are going to a city called Hamadan. We'll live in real

buildings with walls and a roof. Like the schoolroom. No tents. And we'll eat and go to school and play just the way we do here. But it will be better." Anna looked at Samira from where she was helping the little girls pack and shook her head a little.

"It will be better," said Samira again.

Elias nodded and Samira smiled. At least he believed her.

THREE

Not Just Orphans

Hamadan Orphanage
September 1922

BEFORE THE children climbed into the backs of the heavy army trucks, Miss Watson came around.

"It's not far to Hamadan, but we must go over the Assadabad Pass. The road is very steep and you'll have to walk so that the trucks can make it to the top. We'll camp one night along the way." She suddenly smiled a real smile. "You children certainly know how to do that!"

The road was very rough. It seemed to Samira that the truck was leaping over the bumps. The older girls sat as firmly as they could on the benches, each one tightly holding on to a smaller child. They all swayed and bounced as the truck jolted along, churning up dust. Samira covered her mouth with her scarf and squinted to keep as much dust as possible out of her eyes, but she had to keep looking around, too.

The road went along a valley at the bottom of brown mountains. Nothing was green. The grass was dried golden, and the few bushes and trees were as dusty brown as the road. Every now and then they passed a village, but most of the houses were half fallen in, and Samira saw no people in the fields. The war had been here.

Samira had asked one of the teachers at Kermanshah why so many of the villages were ruined.

"Everywhere there was a real road the armies came and villages were fought over," he told her. "People had no choice but to run away, and now they have nothing to come home to. Some of the villages far from roads were not so damaged."

Now Samira thought of Ayna, her village. No one ever drove there in a truck, and it was a long day's walk from the city. Was her house still standing? What would she and Benyamin do if they got to Ayna and the roofs of the houses were caved in and the walls were crumbling?

The truck slowed down. The sound of the motor changed, grinding and struggling. Samira leaned out to see around the cab of the truck. The road ahead was very steep.

The truck stopped and Samira stood up.

"It's time to walk," she said, and all the children jumped down and began to walk beside the road.

It felt good not to be bouncing on a hard bench, and at first they ran and skipped ahead of the trucks. But then the mountain seemed to be holding them back. They began to trudge up the steep slope, and the trucks slowly passed them.

As the last one ground its way past the panting children, Miss Watson waved to them from the window, pointing up ahead.

"We'll wait for you at the top," she called.

Benyamin came and walked beside Samira.

"We're going east," he said. "But if we went north and just a little west and kept going we would come to Ayna."

"Benyamin, don't think about it. We can't do it."

"I know that even better than you," said Benyamin. "But don't forget. We did walk all the way once."

Samira's eyes opened wide. Benyamin was right. They had walked all the way from Ayna to Hamadan that long time ago.

Benyamin reached out to touch her shoulder.

"I can't help thinking about it," he said. "But you don't have to. We'll be safe in Hamadan and we'll see what happens next."

When the children arrived, panting, at the top of the pass, Miss Watson said, "Our documents have been checked and we can go on to our camping place. Tomorrow will be downhill almost all the way."

The next morning the travelers woke very early. They ate bread and hard-boiled eggs and were on their way as the sun rose.

Samira ached all over from the bouncing. Anna wouldn't talk and Elias complained about having to sit down as the truck rolled along. But before the sun was overhead they began to pass houses along the road. They were almost there.

Suddenly there was a shout from the truck ahead. "We have arrived!"

The trucks slowed down and all the children stood up to get a look at their new home. They were approaching a high wall made of mud bricks. There was a wide wooden gate in the wall, and a man appeared and opened it to let the trucks bump into the yard.

Most of the children sat down so they wouldn't fall, but Samira kept a firm hand on Elias's shoulder to steady herself. She had a good view of the orphanage before the truck lurched to a stop.

Celia Barker Lottridge

She saw a group of low gray buildings with small windows like little blind eyes. The earth around the buildings was bare and trampled. The whole place looked lonely and empty of spirit.

The moment the trucks stopped moving, the children jumped out, and suddenly the space was filled with life. The older children stood and looked at the buildings that would be their home, but the younger ones ran and jumped and called to each other.

Miss Watson appeared with a key in her hand and unlocked the door at the end of the nearest building. She turned to Samira and Anna who were standing close by and said, "You can go in if you like."

"We might as well see the worst," said Anna.

Elias came and took Samira's hand and they walked through the door. Before them was a hallway that stretched to the end of the building, with open doors on either side. Elias let go of Samira and ran the whole length of the hall. Then he ran into every room, zigzagging back and forth. She followed slowly.

There wasn't much to see. Every room was exactly the same, square with mud brick walls and one small window that gave a glimpse of the bare yard and the wall with the tops of the mountains beyond it, far away.

Elias ran up to her. "There is a roof and windows just like you said. It's a house for us."

Samira looked at his grubby, shining face and thought, "He can't remember a house with rugs on the floor and cushions and an oven to make it warm. He only remembers tents."

When they were back outside she looked around the empty yard and asked Miss Watson, "Why is everything so bare? People lived here, didn't they?"

"During the war these were barracks where soldiers from India lived. They were part of the British army and they went home when the war ended. The buildings have stood empty for the past four years. Finally the army has decided to give them to us to use for the orphanage."

She sighed. "We would have liked to have the orphanage inside the city walls where there's a school and a hospital, but Hamadan is crowded with thousands of refugees. They ran away from the war, too, and they're still stuck here. There is simply no place in the city to put all of you. We're lucky to have these buildings, and it only takes half an hour to walk into the city."

"The camp was better than this ugly place," Anna said stubbornly.

Miss Watson frowned a little. "When I come back to visit I'm sure everything will look very different."

"You aren't going to stay?"

"Oh, no," said Miss Watson briskly. "I have to go back to Baghdad. I came to help you make the journey. But I'll leave you in good hands. The new director will arrive soon and get things fixed up. In the meantime, Mr. Edwards will be here."

As the children sat on the ground eating their noon meal, Miss Watson told them that five buildings would be used as dormitories. The girls would have three buildings because some of the smallest boys would stay with them.

"Two or three to a room," she said. "I'll assign the rooms

after you eat and then you can get yourselves settled. I'll come by later to see that everything is in order."

Getting settled took only a few minutes. Samira and Anna unrolled the sleeping mats, spread out the quilts and arranged the clothes bundles against the wall, as usual.

When Miss Watson came in she looked at the three beds. "I suppose that soon Elias will go and live with the boys. Do you know how old he is?"

"He was a tiny baby when he came to the camp at Baqubah," said Samira. "He was there for three years, like us, and then he was at Kermanshah."

"So he's about four years old," said Anna.

"Of course," said Miss Watson. "All of you have been in camps for four years. I knew that but I never thought of a child spending his whole life in camps. And you girls were quite young when you had to leave your villages. You must remember very little of your lives before you came to Baqubah."

Samira and Anna didn't say anything. Why should they tell her what they remembered?

Miss Watson glanced around the room again. "You've made it very neat but that floor will need more sweeping. I know the relief people tried to clean this place before you came but it really is disgracefully dusty." She shook her head and went off to check the room next door.

Samira made sure that Miss Watson couldn't hear her before she said, "Miss Watson doesn't know anything about dirt floors, does she?"

"Always dusty," said Anna. "We need rugs, not sweeping."

"I guess we remember something about our lives before

Baqubah," said Samira. "Now let's find Elias. It's bedtime."

The next morning Miss Watson left and Mr. Edwards arrived.

"I'm your director again," he said. "But this time it's definitely temporary. You'll be getting a permanent director before long. But we'll get things started as best we can."

Samira and Anna looked at each other. They could tell he was hoping the new director would arrive soon.

"Mr. Edwards doesn't know what needs to be done for winter," Anna said later. "It's going to be cold and nothing is ready. Not even our feet!"

Samira looked down at her own brown, dirty feet and nodded. The shoes made so long ago in Baghdad had worn out on the stony fields at Kermanshah.

"We just have to wait for the real director," she said. "I hope he knows what to do."

Mr. Edwards did have plans. He asked Benyamin and Ashur to explore and make a list of all the orphanage buildings and what was in them.

"We don't really know what's here except for ten barracks we can use as dormitories," he told them. "I'll tell the caretaker to unlock everything. You take a look and report back to me. I have to get busy organizing supplies." And off he went.

When Samira heard what the boys were doing, she said to Benyamin, "Anna and I will come along. We might see something you miss."

After opening one heavy door after another and walking through dust that hadn't been disturbed for years, they made a list. There was a kitchen with stoves and shelves, a big building that was completely empty, another big building with broken furniture heaped at one end, and two small buildings that looked like houses in a village. One of them had two rooms and the other only one.

When Mr. Edwards read the list he said, "Good. We've got a kitchen and a big room for eating. The other big building will be the schoolroom and recreation room combined. That building with two rooms can be used for the director's office and a place for the doctor and nurse to work. The other can be a store room."

"All these buildings are empty," said Anna. "There's no furniture that isn't broken and we have no rugs or cushions."

"I have a plan about furniture," said Mr. Edwards. "Rugs and cushions will have to wait."

He told the boys to take all the broken furniture into the yard and spread it out. There were banged-up tabletops, chairs with broken legs and many oddly shaped pieces of wood.

"Just junk," said Benyamin, but Mr. Edwards reached into the pile and pulled out a large flat piece of wood.

"We'll make a table out of this," he said. "If there's one thing I know, it's how to build furniture. I used to teach carpentry back home, and now I'll teach you."

He brought back some tools the next time he went into the city, and soon the boys were busy making table legs out of scraps of wood.

"We'll need cupboards for the schoolroom and a few chairs for the teachers," said Mr. Edwards. "Luckily you kids sit on the floor."

September passed, but except for the new furniture Samira saw that most jobs were still being put off until the director came.

"It's October," said Anna one day. "At home we would be almost ready for winter by now. The wheat would be stored and the grapes would be drying. And the grape syrup would be made."

"I know," said Samira. "My father said that a full umbar meant a happy winter. We always had plenty to eat."

She thought of the cellar under the terrace in Ayna. The door was set into the ground and it was too heavy for her to lift, so she never went down without her mother. But when they went down the steep stairs with a lantern to light their way, she was in a magic place. There were bags of wheat and dried beans, oil in jars as tall as she was, dried fruits and pickled vegetables in crocks. It smelled wonderful.

Grape vines heavy with grapes festooned the walls. The grapes dried very slowly under the ground, and the raisins were juicy and delicious. Before Samira and her mother returned to the bright world above, they would pick a few of the grapes and chew them slowly, remembering the summer.

"I think there's an umbar here," Samira said. "People must have lived in those two small buildings before the barracks were built. They would have needed a place to store food."

"People like Mr. Edwards would never think of an umbar," said Anna. "They didn't store food for us in Baqubah or Kermanshah and they won't here. They'll send food in. Endless lentils and onions, probably."

Samira made a face. "It would be better if we had some

food stored up. Something we could count on, the way we did at home. We live here. It should be more like home."

THE TRUTH was that the orphanage didn't feel like home. The rooms were dark and bare. Cold wind from the mountains blew through the open windows. The children shivered under their quilts at night and dressed quickly in the morning to run to the eating room where hot tea and warm bread would be ready for them.

Mr. Edwards kept saying that the director would arrive soon. But the director didn't come.

One morning in the middle of October, Samira woke very early, knowing that something had disturbed her sleep. She listened intently. On one side of her Anna was sleeping quietly, but on the other side Elias was coughing and breathing heavily.

Samira went over to him. He was hot with fever, and she could hear his breath rasping in his throat.

She woke Anna.

"Elias is sick," she said. "Go and get Mr. Edwards."

Mr. Edwards slept in one of the boys' dormitories, in a room right beside the main door. In only a moment he was kneeling by Elias, feeling his forehead.

"You're right," he said. "I'll send the caretaker to the city. I hope the doctor can come very soon. How are you feeling?"

"I'm worried about Elias but I feel fine," said Samira, and Anna said, "Me, too."

"That's good. Stay away from the other children until we find out what this is. But you can fetch some breakfast from the kitchen."

Samira sat down beside Elias. His face was flushed and he muttered in his sleep.

Samira remembered Maryam's face as she lay in their mother's arms. But she was so still. Elias could not be as sick as she was.

The doctor didn't come until nearly noon. Samira made herself busy wiping the little boy's hot face with a damp cloth and keeping the quilt from tangling around him as he moved restlessly. Anna brought her a piece of bread and a bowl of yogurt.

When Samira set them down uneaten, Anna said, "It won't do any good for you to get sick, too. I'm just as worried as you are but remember, Elias is a strong boy and he hasn't been running through the wilderness to save his life."

"I know. I just can't help remembering." Samira leaned back against the wall and ate the food.

When the doctor finally came she waited outside in the corridor with Anna. It seemed a long time before he came out with Mr. Edwards and closed the door.

He smiled at them. "The news is good. Elias is a sick little boy but he doesn't have typhus or any of the dangerous illnesses we watch for."

Samira took a step toward him. "You're sure? He won't…" She stopped.

The doctor looked at her seriously. "No, Elias won't die. He'll be miserable for a few days but he will get well. I'm wondering whether you two girls would look after him? The important thing is to keep him in bed and give him plenty of cool, weak tea to drink. Moving him all the way to the hospital wouldn't help."

When both girls nodded he went on, "Take turns being with him. I don't want either one of you to get worn out and pick up what he has. I'll be back tomorrow to see how he's doing. If he's sicker I'll take him to the hospital."

When the doctor was gone, Samira said to Anna, "I'd like to stay with Elias until I can see that he's better. I can't help thinking of Maryam."

Anna nodded. "I'll take my mat into that empty room down the hall and get a good sleep tonight. Then I'll be ready for Elias when he's feeling better."

For the rest of the afternoon Samira sat on her mat and watched Elias sleep. She gave him tea to drink when he woke for a few minutes and sang softly to help him sleep again. By nightfall she thought he was breathing more easily, and she fell asleep herself.

The window was gray with early morning light when she woke up.

"Are you sick, too?" a scratchy voice said. "I've asked and asked for a drink."

She leaned over to look at him closely. His eyes were still bright with fever and he hadn't bothered to sit up, but there was determination in his voice.

"He's getting better," she said to herself, feeling that she had woken from a nightmare.

"No, I'm not sick," she said. "I'll get you a drink."

When the doctor came back he said that Elias definitely was getting better.

"He doesn't need to go to the hospital, but he must stay in bed until his fever is gone."

The next two days weren't difficult. Elias was glad to lie in bed as the girls sang to him and told him stories. Then he began to feel better and it was a challenge just to keep him quiet. Samira had to keep telling herself how glad she was that he was not limp and feverish anymore.

On the fourth morning it was her turn to look after him until lunchtime. He was hardly coughing at all and he wanted a new story, an exciting one. Samira had eaten bread and cheese for breakfast but she was hungry.

"Once there was a boy who was hungry..." she started.

"That's not exciting," said Elias.

"Listen," said Samira. "This boy was hungry for something extra good, something very special. He heard about an umbar, a cellar, where all sorts of wonderful food was kept. Honey and rock sugar and fruit. It was a magic umbar where he could find anything he wanted to eat."

She paused. How would the boy find this umbar? Elias was looking at her, waiting.

Just then she heard voices in the hall. Who could it be? All the children were in school. Samira forgot about the hungry boy. She got up and went to the door.

A woman wearing trousers and a jacket was walking down the hall with Mr. Edwards, talking quietly. Her hair was short and brown. Samira couldn't see her face, but she could hear her voice, asking questions.

Elias got up and pushed himself in front of her so that he could see, too. Samira put her finger to her lips.

"Shhh. Be very, very quiet. Mr. Edwards has a guest and we mustn't disturb them."

Elias looked up at her and said, "Shhhhh."

Celia Barker Lottridge

Samira patted his shoulder. By listening hard she could catch a word now and then.

"Windows," the woman said. And "cold" and "winter" and "wheat."

Mr. Edwards kept shaking his head. Samira knew what that meant. He was saying that nothing had been done about the winter. No window coverings, no wheat stored up.

About halfway down the hall the woman turned and saw the two children in the doorway. She smiled and came toward them.

"This must be your room," she said. "What are your names?"

"I'm Samira and this is Elias."

"Is he your brother?"

"No. He's just little so Anna and I look after him," said Samira.

"That's like being a sister."

"Yes, it is," said Samira. "And I have a real brother, too. Benyamin. He's older than I am. He lives in the boys' dormitory."

"You're lucky to have two kinds of brothers," said the woman. "Now I'll know who Benyamin is when I meet him." She paused. "I should tell you who I am. I'm Miss Shedd. I've come to be the director of the orphanage. I was just telling Mr. Edwards that there's a lot to be done. We're all going to be very busy."

Samira couldn't think of a word to say, and she couldn't stop staring. Miss Shedd was young, much younger than Miss Watson or Mrs. McDowell. She wore trousers. And she was the director.

Miss Shedd saw her surprise and looked at her very seriously. "I probably don't look like the director you expected. You see, I came all the way from Tabriz on horseback, and these are my traveling clothes. When I got to Hamadan this morning I wanted to see the orphanage right away. I thought the dormitories would be empty at this hour. Please don't tell the other children about the trousers. Next time you see me I'll be wearing a skirt and look the way a director should." She smiled and Samira had to smile back.

"I won't tell anyone," she promised.

Miss Shedd said, "Thank you, Samira." She looked down at Elias. "Young man, why are you in your sleeping shirt at this hour of the morning? Are you sick? Should I send you back to bed?"

She knelt down and took Elias's face between her hands and looked into his eyes. Then she stood up.

"He has been sick, hasn't he?" she said to Samira.

"He had a fever and sickness in his chest. Anna and I have been looking after him."

"He's better now," said Miss Shedd. "I've had some training as a nurse and I can't detect any fever and he's breathing properly. You've taken good care of him but he should have been in the infirmary." She turned toward Mr. Edwards, who simply shook his head.

"Another thing that hasn't been done yet, I suppose. Well, we'd better get to work." She looked at the children again. "Elias, you listen to Samira and get well." And she walked away down the hall with Mr. Edwards.

Samira felt as if the air around her was crackling with

Miss Shedd's energy. She couldn't wait to tell Anna about the new director. Of course, she couldn't tell everything, she reminded herself. She had to keep her promise.

But Miss Shedd had not made Elias promise. The minute Anna came in he said, "I saw a lady wearing trousers. She said I'm not sick anymore."

"It must have been a dream," said Anna. "Ladies wear skirts."

"No. A lady came. She talked to Samira. She wore trousers. Just like Mr. Edwards."

Anna looked at Samira. "What's he talking about? Is he seeing things? Is he worse?"

"No, he's better." She came close to Anna and spoke in a very low voice. "Look, it's a secret, but a lady did come with Mr. Edwards to look at the dormitory and she was wearing trousers. But that's not important. What's important is that she's the new director of the orphanage."

"Are you telling me that it's a secret that the director has come?" asked Anna.

"That's not the secret. Just the trousers are a secret. We happened to see her in her traveling clothes because she came from Tabriz on horseback. After this she'll wear a skirt like the other ladies. But she's not like the other ladies, Anna. She speaks Syriac almost the way we do and she could see that nothing is ready for winter. She told Mr. Edwards that something must be done."

"Well, I hope I meet her soon, no matter what she's wearing. We need a director," said Anna.

Elias spent the rest of the day telling Anna about the lady who wore trousers. But by the next day when the doctor came to see him, he had forgotten all about her in his eagerness to get outside and play with his friends.

"I feel fine," he said, taking a deep breath through his nose. "See, I can breathe!"

"You are fine, Elias," said the doctor. "You go on outside and play."

He checked Samira and Anna, too.

"No problem with either of you. But get some rest. You've done a big job keeping a little boy quiet."

Several days passed and Miss Shedd did not come to the orphanage again. Now Samira began to worry. Maybe the people in Hamadan had sent her away because of the trousers. Or maybe they thought she wanted too many things for the orphanage and wouldn't let her come back.

But Miss Shedd did come back. One day Samira came out of the eating room after breakfast to find the yard filled with wagons. The drivers were unloading rolled-up rugs and big crates. Walking around supervising everything was Miss Shedd. She was wearing a brown skirt and a bright red jacket.

"She looks so serious," Samira whispered to Anna. "When I saw her before she looked excited and glad to be here."

"She told you that there's a lot to be done, didn't she?" said Anna. "She's getting started."

Miss Shedd was busy counting boxes. When she saw the big boys and girls watching, she called, "Come on over and give me a hand."

The children came closer but they stood a respectful distance away.

"Not over there," she said sharply. "Right here. Two by two. I'll tell you what to take and where it goes."

Celia Barker Lottridge

In no time at all Samira and Anna found themselves carrying a rolled-up rug into each dormitory room. The boys lugged pots and pans and dishes into the kitchen and big boxes of cloth into the school building.

As the children worked, word spread that this woman was the new orphanage director.

At last there was nothing left except six sewing machines standing in a row. Miss Shedd motioned to Benyamin and Ashur.

"These are heavy," she said. "Can you two carry them to the schoolroom?"

The boys nodded.

"Good," said Miss Shedd. "But don't drop them. These machines must be treated with great respect. After all, they'll keep you warm this winter."

By the time all the supplies were in their proper places, every older child had met Miss Shedd.

"She doesn't wait even a second before she tells you to hurry up," complained Anna as they went into the eating hall for lunch. "I need time to get started."

"She's the same with everyone," said Samira. "She told one of the oxcart drivers to move his cart quickly or winter would catch up with him. She's in a hurry to get things done."

"Maybe," said Anna. "Or maybe she's just bossy."

Before the children were dismissed after their meal, Miss Shedd came in and stood at the front of the room. She looked around the room at the children sitting on the floor.

Elias was right in the front. Samira could see him staring hard at Miss Shedd.

Suddenly his voice rang out in the silent room.

"I saw you before," he said. "You were wearing trousers."

Before Samira could take a breath, Miss Shedd said, "Well, I saw you, too. And you were wearing a shirt that came right down to your feet." Then she laughed and everyone laughed with her, though they had no idea what Miss Shedd and Elias were talking about.

Miss Shedd went on, "Children, we have so much to do but we need to laugh, too. Thank you. I am Susan Shedd and I am now the orphanage director. For me coming to this orphanage is a little like coming home. You see, I was born in Urmieh. My father was with the American Mission in the city and I lived there until I was fifteen years old. Then I went to America to go to school. Now I've had the chance to return to Persia and be with you.

"I've been away for a long time but I remember how hard everyone in Urmieh and the villages worked to be ready for winter. This orphanage is new and there hasn't been time to get everything ready, though the cold weather is already here. We have a lot to do very fast. We must make clothes and shoes, store food and make your rooms comfortable. And at the same time you must go to school. We will not let your education fall behind, for you'll need it when you're back in your village or wherever you go in the world."

Samira felt dizzy. She remembered how a gust of wind would suddenly blow down the streets of Ayna, lifting the leaves that lay peacefully on the ground and swirling them high into the air. Now she felt like one of those leaves.

Miss Shedd was still talking. While she talked she was looking around the room, and Samira had the feeling that she was noticing every single child and deciding what task each one would do.

"Until things are in order we will have school in the morning and jobs in the afternoon. Once everything is organized there will be time for afternoon classes and games and music. It won't be all work, I promise, but the work must come first. I want each of you to go to your room in the dormitory. You will find a rug there and some other supplies. You can arrange things as you wish. Just be sure that everyone who lives in the room is pleased with it. Stay in your room until I come around to see how you've settled in. Now, off with you!"

She turned quickly and walked out the door.

Samira looked over at Anna. "Let's get Elias and go and look at our rug. I hope it's red."

The rug turned out to be dark red with a pattern of blue diamonds and a golden brown border. In some places it was very worn, but the girls agreed that it was beautiful, and it felt soft and warm under their bare feet.

Elias immediately lay down on his stomach on the rug. He took a small stick from his pocket and began tracing the blue shapes against the red background, humming quietly.

"I remember doing that," Samira said, almost to herself.

"Let's see what else there is to arrange," said Anna. "I want to be ready when Miss Shedd comes."

There were three cotton quilts and three baskets to hold the clothes they weren't wearing. And there was a metal lantern with a candle in it. It had a loop at the top so that it could be hung from a hook in the wall, if there had been a hook.

They put their extra clothes in the baskets and set the baskets against the wall along with the folded quilts so that they would have the whole rug to play on. Since there was no hook for the lantern, they put it in a corner.

Samira looked around the little room. It held everything that was theirs and they could sit comfortably together on the rug. She sat down beside Elias, who was busy finding many diamond shapes, little and big, in the pattern.

Anna watched for a moment. Then she went outside and came back with several roundish pebbles. Samira knew at once what those pebbles were for.

Anna showed Elias the big blue diamond in the middle of the rug.

"All the pebbles go here," she said. "Now, pick the one you like best and Samira and I will choose, too."

Elias spent a long time choosing the best pebble.

"Now what?" he asked.

"Put your pebble down on the rug and flick it with your finger, like this." She showed him how to flick his first finger against his thumb to make the pebble move across the rug.

Elias's short fingers were surprisingly strong, and soon his pebble was shooting straight and far.

"Now," said Anna, "flick your pebble at those pebbles inside the diamond. If you hit one and it goes out of the diamond, then it's yours. We'll take turns and whoever gets the most pebbles out of the diamond wins."

This was harder. Elias managed to hit one pebble out of the blue diamond and was so pleased that he didn't notice that Anna and Samira were sneaking back the ones they hit so that they wouldn't win too fast. In the end Anna couldn't help winning, but Elias promised her that he would practice and beat her next time.

"He probably will," said Samira. "He's a very determined boy."

Miss Shedd came by as they were gathering up the stones.

"I used to play something like that," she said. "And there's another game where you toss a stone in the air and pick up others as fast as you can."

"Yes," said Samira. "First you throw down all the stones except one." She could remember how the other girls always watched closely to be sure you tossed the stones and didn't just drop them in a heap.

"That's it," said Miss Shedd. "Now, what were the words we said?"

"It's *shkelta* when you throw them and *metaytah* when you pick them up. But you have to get them all up before the stone you tossed comes down," said Samira.

"Oh, yes. I remember." Miss Shedd glanced around the room. "You'll need a hook for the lantern to keep it away from anything that might catch fire. And you'll need some hooks for clothes, too." She smiled. "Don't worry. You'll have new clothes to hang up as fast as we can make them. Shoes, too. Winter's coming, you know." She gave the uncovered window a quick glance, shook her head and was gone.

THREE DAYS later Miss Shedd made an announcement as the children were finishing lunch.

"For a few weeks this eating room will also be the school-room, and the schoolroom will become a workshop for making clothes and shoes. Some of you will be helping with that work. If you are not on the list, don't worry. The rest of you will have other jobs."

She took a piece of paper out of the bag she always carried with her and read the names of girls and boys who would go immediately to the schoolroom. Samira's name was on the list. She walked over to the schoolroom with the three other girls who were to become seamstresses.

"She looks at you with that look and decides that you can sew," one girl grumbled. "I can patch a hole in a shirt but I can't make anything."

"We'll have to learn," said another. "We have to do what she says."

"It might save us from kitchen duty for a while," said Samira.

The other girls brightened up. Kitchen duty meant chopping endless onions and stirring rice so it wouldn't burn and scrubbing out pots. The girls didn't like it and the boys hated it, but now that Miss Shedd was in charge everyone had to take a turn unless they were doing some other urgent task.

When the girls entered the schoolroom they stopped and stared. The shelves of books, the blackboard and the mats where the children sat to do their lessons were gone. At one end of the room three women stood behind a big table heaped with cloth. The sewing machines were lined up and ready to go. At the other end of the room two men were sorting through tools and pieces of canvas cut into squares.

Samira went over to the women. One was old with gray hair. The other two were not old, though they were thin and worn. They all looked very happy.

"You will be helping us make new clothes for everyone," said the gray-haired woman. "I am Hanna, this is Zora and this is Britha. We are refugees like you but we have been in Hamadan all this time living on the little the British gave us. Miss Shedd has blessed us by giving us some work."

Zora was looking at the dress Samira was wearing. She shook her head.

"You won't live through the winter in that," she said. "It gets cold here, you know. You need a nice thick skirt and a blouse and a warm jacket."

Samira believed her. She was wearing the dress that had been made for the heat of Baghdad. Her other dress was warmer, but the cloth was getting thin at the elbows. It had been somebody else's dress for a long time before it was given to her in Kermanshah. As for her warm jacket, she had mended it so often it was hard to put a patch on it anymore.

"Warm clothes will be wonderful," she said. "Will we have new shoes, too?"

"Yes, the men down at the other end are shoemakers," said Britha. "Some boys will work with them and every one of you will have the shoes and clothes you need if we just get to work."

Hanna laughed. "We'll all work," she said. "Susan Shedd won't rest until every last child is properly dressed."

Samira was surprised. "Do you know Miss Shedd? She hasn't been here very long."

"I knew her when she was a girl, living with her family in Urmieh," said Hanna. "She was just as determined then as she is now. She asked for a horse so she could explore outside the city walls. Of course she was never allowed to go unless her father or some other man could go with her but she never gave up asking."

"She told us she went to America when she was fifteen," said Samira.

"Yes, people who came from America to work in the mission always sent their children back there to go to school when they were old enough to live so far away from their families. Susan Shedd hated to leave Urmieh, but she had no choice. Of course, being in America meant that she missed the war, so maybe she was lucky. I never thought I'd see her again but I should have known she would come back and do something useful. And now that she's here she'll expect us to be working, not talking. Let's get started."

They got to work. Samira remembered watching the women in Baghdad make the green dresses on sewing machines, but she had not used the machines herself.

"Look," said Hanna. "You turn the wheel with your right hand so that the needle goes up and down. You guide the cloth under the needle with your left hand."

Samira found that sewing on a machine wasn't hard as long as she kept her eye on the line of stitches. It had to be straight. If the seam was crooked she had to rip it out and stitch it again.

Anna was not sewing. She was learning how to take care of babies. It seemed that there were some Assyrian orphans in Hamadan, most of them very young. They would be coming from the nursery in Hamadan to live at the orphanage soon.

"But these babies weren't even born until after the war was over," Samira said. "How did they come to be orphans?"

"Miss Shedd says it's been very hard here," Anna replied. "Some people were weak and sick when they came and they didn't survive. Like Elias's mother. Miss Shedd says we have to do our best to give these babies a good life."

Samira felt a little jealous of Anna. Taking care of orphan babies was surely more important than sewing clothes. Then one afternoon Miss Shedd came to the sewing room.

"Without warm clothes and sturdy shoes children will be cold. Some might get sick," she said. "So I'm counting on you to do your work well." She smiled. "I would even say that what you are making is essential to the children's survival, at least to their healthy survival."

Essential to our survival. Samira liked those words. She repeated them and wiggled her toes inside her new flannel-lined shoes as she watched the sewing-machine needle go up and down. She was making a pair of blue trousers for a little boy. When she came to the end of the seam she held them up. They were thick and warm and the seams were straight.

"These trousers would fit Elias," she thought. "Maybe they would even help him survive." She decided to sew a pocket on each side so that the little boy who wore them could keep his hands warm, too.

Benyamin and Ashur had been given the task of weighing each load of wood, charcoal and wheat brought to the orphanage on mules. The mule drivers unloaded the bundles or bags and the boys weighed them in a big scale that dangled from a post in the yard.

Miss Shedd was there to record the weight of every load so she could pay the men exactly the right amount. Some of them argued with her, wanting more money, but she never gave in. She pointed to the figures she had written down. The men stared at the numbers. None of them could read, but they shook their heads and argued some more. Then she told them that the orphanage could only deal with honest suppliers. If they wanted more business they should take their payment and go.

"She never shouts but she never backs down," Benyamin told Samira. "And she's a woman. The men are very surprised." He shook his head. Samira thought he was surprised, too.

The boys stacked the wood and charcoal and covered the stacks with canvas. They carried sacks of wheat into the schoolroom and piled them between the sewing and the shoemaking. Then they put big trays on the floor and emptied grain onto each one. Eight women came to clean the grain and each had one of the younger children working next to her. They had quick fingers and sharp eyes, Miss Shedd said.

Their job was to look through the grain and pick out pebbles and chunks of mud. Once in a while one of the children forgot and tossed a pebble at another child, only to have his hand slapped by the woman beside him.

When the grain was clean, the boys poured it back into the sacks and took it to the storage building, where it stayed until it was taken to the mill to be ground into flour.

One afternoon after Samira had been sewing for several hours, Hanna said, "You've done enough for today. I brought some almond cakes. Take one for yourself and one for your brother, too."

Samira took the small golden cakes and thanked Hanna. This was a real treat. Something a little sweet with the rich taste of almonds. She nibbled on her cake and went in search of Benyamin.

He wasn't hard to find. He was sweeping loose dirt out the door of the little storage building and was happy to stop.

"This floor isn't just dirt," he said. "I've found a part that's made of wood."

Samira handed him the almond cake and went to look. Houses never had wood floors.

She bent over the place where Benyamin had swept away a thick layer of dirt. The wood underneath was old and splintered. With her fingertips she scraped away more dirt and found a small round hole that might have been made by a nail.

"Benyamin, come and look! I think there was a handle here. This isn't a floor. It could be the door to an umbar."

Benyamin came and squatted down. His fingers found three more holes.

"You're right," he said. "The handle is long gone but it's definitely a door."

"Can we open it?"

"Not by ourselves. It will have to be pried up. I'll go and tell Miss Shedd."

Miss Shedd came at once.

"An umbar! I hope you're right, Samira. We need more space for our winter food supplies." She stopped for a moment, looking at nothing in particular. "I remember going into the umbar at the mission with my mother and sneaking some almonds while she scooped wheat from the big sack." She gave her head a little shake. "Go and tell the men who are unloading wood for the window frames that we need them to come with a crowbar and a lantern."

When the door was pried up, Miss Shedd lit the lantern and held it over the hole in the floor. They could all see stairs leading down into darkness.

"We have to go down," she said. "I'll go first to be sure it's safe."

In a few moments they heard her voice echoing beneath them.

"It's an umbar, all right. A big one," she said. "It has an earth ledge around the sides and there are some old clay jars. Empty, of course."

She came back up the stairs. "Someone must have lived in this house long ago. The Hindu soldiers never knew. But now we know and we have plenty of things to store in an umbar. Do you want to take a look? After all, you found it."

Samira followed Benyamin carefully down the steps that were cut into the earth. She remembered how high each step was in the umbar at home and how her mother held the lamp so she wouldn't stumble. These steps were much lower.

No, she was much taller, and it was Benyamin holding the light.

"Don't be disappointed," he said. "There's nothing here."

Samira knew he was thinking of all the dried fruit and grain and oil that had been in their umbar when they had to leave the village.

"The people who lived here were lucky," she said. "They took everything with them."

Benyamin swung the beam of the lantern around the

room. A round shape caught Samira's eye. Something was buried in the earthen floor.

"Bring the light over here," she said and knelt to look closely. The thing she had found was small, no bigger across than the palm of her hand, and made of dull metal.

"It's not a golden treasure," said Benyamin. She scrabbled in the dirt and finally dug up a shallow metal cup. It was badly dented, but Samira knew what it was.

"It's a measure," she said. "For measuring out something like pepper or cloves." She held its round shape in her hand. She could imagine a woman coming down into the umbar and scooping out spices. Then one day she dropped the measure and never came back to get it.

Samira turned back to the stairs and was glad to get up into the light.

Miss Shedd looked carefully at the metal cup. "I agree with you. It's a measure. Would you like to keep it? It should be yours."

"Yes," said Samira. She took the little cup and held it carefully in her hand.

Miss Shedd set the wooden door over the stairs. "We'll fill this umbar with the food we need for the winter," she said. "And I promise you that when we leave we'll take everything with us. The umbar will be left empty for someone else to use."

Samira stared at her. "Leave? Are we going to leave? Will we have to go to another orphanage?"

Miss Shedd frowned a little. "We'll only leave when I've figured out a way to get you home."

"I want to go home," said Samira slowly. "But I saw

ruined villages along the road when we came here. Our house might be falling down and we are orphans. How can we go home?"

Now Miss Shedd really looked at Samira and at Benyamin standing behind her.

"I know that your parents are gone," she said gently. "But I'm sure that most of you have relatives or even family friends who would be glad take you into their families, maybe in a nearby village. That's the way the Assyrian people are. I just have to figure out how you can get there."

Miss Shedd went on, but now she seemed to be talking to herself. "The problem is I could never get enough horses and wagons to carry everyone. Or even mules."

Benyamin took a step forward. "Miss Shedd, we don't need wagons." Then he said again what he had said to Samira when they were leaving Kermanshah. "Most of us walked from beyond Lake Urmieh to Hamadan four years ago when we had to run from our villages." He took a deep breath. "None of us want to make a journey like that one again, but we walked all the way."

Miss Shedd looked at Benyamin for a long time. She nodded once.

Then she said, "Yes. You walked. I won't forget."

LIFE IN the Hamadan Orphanage went on as if the children would be there forever. Every child was busy learning to read, practicing writing, stitching clothes, making shoes, storing food and doing the regular chores of cooking and cleaning.

Carpenters from the city had finished making frames for windows in the dormitories and were ready to put them into the openings. Samira was hoping for glass windows. She had never seen one until she went to the orphanage in Baghdad. But the day the windows went in she saw that the Hamadan orphanage would have to make do with thin fabric stretched tightly inside the window frames.

"At least the cloth is white," she said to Anna. "It lets some light through and it will keep out the worst of the cold wind."

Next, eight women from the city took over the sewing space and began to stitch rolls of wool batting into thick warm quilts. They could sew much faster than the girls, and winter would not wait. Quilts piled up at one end of the room. At the other the shoemakers kept making more and more shoes.

"Why so many shoes?" said Anna one day. "Every one of us has a new pair already."

"There are more than one hundred pairs sitting there," said Samira. "I counted. I'm very sure Miss Shedd has a plan for those shoes."

One morning after lessons Miss Shedd told them who would wear the shoes. "All of you children came from the Baqubah camp," she said. "Now one hundred and fifty children from other camps will be joining us here. Because of all our hard work we're prepared for them. The rooms in the empty dormitories are ready and we have plenty of food stored. Fortunately these children already have new clothing so we didn't have to make extra."

"And we have shoes waiting for them," Samira whispered to Anna.

Miss Shedd heard her. "You're very observant. We made

extra shoes for the new children. But there is one thing we don't have. Our schoolroom is not big enough to hold all of you plus the new children. So starting tomorrow if you are ten years old or older you will go the Assyrian school in the city. You'll walk down the hill in the morning and up the hill at night. Girls on one side of the road and boys on the other. Mr. Althius, who will be teaching the boys, will go with you. I count on all of you to behave well and study hard. I also expect you to welcome the new children to Hamadan Orphanage when they arrive in four or five days. Please make them feel at home and help them get settled here."

She pointed to a big piece of brown wrapping paper she had tacked to the wall.

"There's one more job to be done. With the new people coming I think we need some rules written down so that they will know what's expected of them. If you think of a good rule, write it here." She stopped and smiled. "Now, for the very first time since I have been your director, I can say, 'There's no work to be done. Go outside and play!'"

Before they went out, Samira and Anna and Benyamin and Ashur looked at the big piece of paper.

"There's room for a lot of rules," said Anna. "Why does she want us to make up rules, anyway? Teachers and people like that make up rules."

"Miss Shedd wants us to think," said Samira. "If we just hear the rules or read them we won't think about them."

"I don't want to think about rules," said Ashur. "I want to start up a game out in the yard."

He led the way outside. The yard was still bare but there were a few benches against the school building and a big box

Celia Barker Lottridge

with balls in it. Ashur grabbed one of the balls and the boys began to kick it around. The younger children were playing tag.

Samira joined the other girls on a bench and looked around the yard. She knew every single child. They had been together in Baqubah and Baghdad and Kermanshah, and they had all worked to make the Hamadan Orphanage a good place to live.

"This yard feels like our yard," she thought. "Pretty soon dozens of children we don't know will be playing here, too. It will change everything."

The next day Mr. Althius counted the children lined up beside the orphanage gate. There were forty-five girls and thirty-nine boys.

"When the other children arrive there will be twice as many," he said. "I'm counting on you to walk in an orderly fashion today and every day. We want the city of Hamadan to be glad we're here. So, no trouble. Is that understood?"

When they reached the city Samira decided that Hamadan didn't give much possibility for trouble. The street took them between mud brick houses with no windows in the outer walls. If there was a marketplace she didn't see it. Mr. Althius led them straight to a building that was strange because it was not all on one floor. There were two rows of windows, one above the other.

"This is the school," said Mr. Althius. "The boys will be on the second floor and the girls on the first. You girls who are thirteen or older go to the room on the right and the rest go to the one on the left."

Samira went with Anna. In the classroom, Miss Shuman greeted them.

"Please sit around these tables and tell me your names. I want to be sure that each of you is in the right class."

They spent the day reading paragraphs and answering questions about what they had read. Miss Shuman dictated a piece from a story and everyone wrote it down. Samira knew that she had done as well as most of the girls and better than some.

Then Miss Shulman put some arithmetic problems on the blackboard.

"I'd like you to copy these into your notebooks and solve them," she said.

Adding up numbers was not hard for Samira, and she could figure out subtraction, but there were multiplication problems on the board. The only way she could solve them was by counting on her fingers.

Miss Shulman called her up to her desk. "I see that you have not studied multiplication, Samira. You'll have to spend extra time memorizing the times tables. Are you willing to do that? In every other subject you fit into this class."

"I'll work hard on multiplication," Samira promised.

"Very well, then. I'll see you tomorrow."

After the evening meal Miss Shedd gathered a few of the children and said, "That piece of paper I put up yesterday has no writing on it. You've had a day to think about rules and I'd like to see some ideas up here before you go out to play."

The boys and girls stared at the piece of paper. They had lived with many rules in the camps. No talking once the lamps were out. Divide food equally. Stay in line when going between tents. No running except when playing games.

The list was long. But no one had ever asked them to think up even one rule themselves.

Finally Ashur said what they were all thinking. "We know what we're supposed to do. The other kids will know, too. What good will it do to write rules down?"

"It's only fair to let the new children know what is expected in this orphanage," said Miss Shedd. "But I agree that rules saying 'do this' and 'don't do that' are not very inspiring. So think about what would make your life here happy. Or what would make it unhappy so that you would like it never to happen. Turn those thoughts into rules." She looked around at all of them. "I have things to do. I'm going to leave you to it."

When she was gone Anna said, "Since we have to do this, I'll say that it would make my life happier if the boys would not try to get out of kitchen duty. I'm always having to find a boy who's sneaking away hoping someone else will wash the dishes."

"So each person should be responsible for checking the job schedule and showing up for their job," said Benyamin, and he picked up a pencil and wrote down rule number one.

Ashur said, "I want a rule that says the north end of the yard is for games with balls. Right now the little kids get under our feet as soon as we start kicking the ball around." He wrote his rule down.

Farah, who never said anything in a group, stepped forward and picked up the pencil. She wrote, *No calling people mean names.* Samira knew why. Farah was a round girl and sometimes people called after her, "Fatty fatty Farah."

"That's Farah's rule," thought Samira. "What rule do I want?" But she couldn't think of even one.

Anna whispered in her ear, "Your turn. Think of a rule, Samira."

Suddenly Samira remembered that Anna had been the first girl to speak to her in Baqubah. She remembered Anna's voice and Anna's hand reaching out to her when she hadn't been able to speak to anyone for days.

She took the pencil and wrote, *Be friendly to strangers who come to our orphanage. Don't let them be alone.*

When the children came through the orphanage gate after school the next day, Samira heard the sound of many voices. The yard was crowded with children of all sizes. They were standing in clumps, some near the wall and others over by the eating room. In one group every child was dressed in dark blue. Another group wore khaki. Some children were barefoot and others wore patched shoes tied on with bits of string.

"Look," she said to Anna. "You can see that they come from different camps. And Miss Shedd was right about their shoes."

Miss Shedd was going from group to group. After she had spoken with a group for a few minutes they picked up their bundles and went to one of the dormitories.

"They're going to get settled," said Anna. "Next time we see them they'll be wearing the shoes our boys made."

As soon as all the newcomers had gone off with their bundles, Miss Shedd came over and joined the children waiting by the gate.

"This has happened a few days earlier than I expected," she said. "I wanted to plan a good welcome for these children but I haven't even worked out the meal schedule yet. There's no way everyone can eat at once, so tonight you'll be

Celia Barker Lottridge

eating first and the new children will have their turn after they get their rooms settled." She shook her head and went off quickly.

At supper Samira found herself eating very fast, thinking that the new children would be hungry after their journey. She wasn't the only one. The dishes were cleared away and washed in record time and everyone hurried out. They stood around the yard trying not to stare as the newcomers went in to eat.

Samira wondered what would happen when they came out. But nothing happened. The new children came out of the eating room and walked straight to their dormitories. There was no chance to speak to even one of them.

At breakfast the next day all of the children who went into town for school ate at the same time, but the newcomers came in as a group and sat at one end of the eating hall. On the way down the hill Samira tried to talk to two girls wearing green, but they turned away and went on with their own conversation.

She said to Anna, "I thought my rule was a good one but how can I be friendly to people who won't even look at me?"

Anna, as always, was practical. "We all live together in the orphanage. Eventually they'll have to talk to us."

Miss Shuman welcomed the new girls to her classroom. "Today I'll be working with you to see where you fit in. You other girls can go over yesterday's lessons."

One of the new girls in Miss Shuman's class was named Maryam. Samira thought she looked younger than thirteen and she was sitting by herself, not with the other new girls.

When they all went out into the schoolyard for their morning break, Maryam sat on a bench in the sun. Samira sat beside her and offered her some dried apricots she had saved from breakfast.

"Thank you," said Maryam.

They were both silent for a minute. Then Samira said, "This is the first school I've been to. Of course we had lessons in the camp at Baqubah but before that I didn't go to school at all. Did you?"

"Oh, yes," said Maryam. "Our village is quite close to the city so my mother got a teacher to come to our house for me and my sister, so we could learn to read. Later my father walked with us twice a week to a girls' school in a bigger village. We were going to go to the school in the city, but then…"

Samira knew that Maryam didn't want to talk about what had happened when the war came, so she asked the first question that came into her head. "How old are you now?"

"I'm just about to turn thirteen. I know I'm a little young for the senior class but I wouldn't fit in the junior class. That's what Miss Shuman said."

Samira smiled at her. "I'm one of the youngest in the class and there are things I have to catch up on. We'll be the junior members of the senior class, all right?"

"All right," said Maryam, and Samira felt that this girl was no longer a stranger.

On the way back to the orphanage Maryam walked with Samira and Anna, but most of the newcomers were still walking together, avoiding the Baqubah children.

Mr. Althius moved along the line, but when he was out of sight some of the boys stumbled on purpose into boys walking near them. One swung his arm and hit Ashur across the back. The teacher came just in time to stop a fight from breaking out.

Maryam was asking Samira what jobs she had around the orphanage when she suddenly fell silent. Samira looked around and saw that some of the new girls behind them were whispering together and looking at Maryam and rolling their eyes.

Suddenly Anna said, "Look!" She pulled Samira around to see a boy, a newcomer, running down the road toward the end of the line. Some boys tried to trip him as he went past, but he dodged them and ran on.

Maryam watched him go and shook her head.

"That's Malik," she said. "He was in the Mosul camp with us but he goes off by himself whenever he can. He always comes back, so most of us just let him go."

"Why does he run?" asked Anna.

"I don't know, but he wants to be away from everyone else. He doesn't talk much and he can run really fast. That's all I know."

By now they had reached the orphanage gate. Miss Shedd was waiting for them and, as usual, she seemed to see everything. She was going over to some boys who had been pushing and jostling the boys ahead of them, when Malik came running through the gate.

"It's the wild one," shouted a voice. Two boys broke away from the group and began chasing Malik, who dodged behind one of the dormitory buildings.

Miss Shedd walked to the middle of the yard and stood perfectly still. She motioned to the other children to stay where they were, in a group, blocking the gate.

Samira knew that Malik had no way to get out of the orphanage compound. He was surrounded by walls and she suddenly felt sad for him. She was sure that walls didn't make him feel safe. They made him feel trapped.

The boys who had run after Malik came back panting. The taller one said defiantly, "We couldn't find him."

"I didn't ask you to find him," said Miss Shedd calmly. "He'll show up when he's ready. As for you, I want both of you to come with me right now."

She cast her eyes over the motionless group of children and saw Samira and Anna standing with Maryam.

"You three come as well. And you, Ashur, and the boy behind you, come along."

Samira saw that the boy who followed Ashur was the one who had hit him on the way up the hill. He came and stood a distance from Miss Shedd with his arms tight by his sides and his shoulders very square.

"Tell me your name," she said.

"Avram," said the boy.

"I'll be meeting with these boys and girls," Miss Shedd said to the whole group. "You'll hear about our discussion later. Now you are free to play or go to your rooms and do school work."

She turned and led the seven baffled children toward her office. Samira could hear a hum of talk beginning behind her. She, too, wondered what Miss Shedd was going to do.

They all filed into the office and Miss Shedd shut the door. Samira could see a desk with a hard wooden chair behind it, shelves crowded with books, and a soft chair covered with a brightly colored shawl.

On the desk were many pieces of paper, some in piles and some scattered. There was an inkwell with a pen sticking out of it.

But what Samira noticed most was a photograph of a man with dark eyes and a dark beard.

As Miss Shedd sat down at the desk she saw Samira looking at the picture.

"My father," she said. "I like to think he knows about my work."

Samira nodded. Miss Shedd's father must be gone, like Papa. His eyes in the picture looked sad and kind.

Miss Shedd was speaking to everyone. She didn't sound angry.

"Please sit down," she said. "There's room for all of you on the rug."

When they were all sitting she went on. "Some of you have been in this orphanage for nearly two months. We know each other and we've learned how to get along together. Those of you who arrived yesterday don't know me yet and I don't know you. But I do know that we cannot live here with any happiness if people fight or are unkind to each other. Tell me what happened just now. You must have had a reason for chasing that boy."

She waited. The silence went on and on until it seemed to be stealing air from the room.

Then the smaller boy who had chased Malik spoke.

"It's that kid," he said. "Malik. He won't talk to us. He always runs off by himself. He never plays ball with us. I think he hates us so we hate him."

"But he doesn't harm you and he always comes back."

"Yes," said the boy.

"Then leave him alone. We don't know why he runs but we'll never find out if people chase him. Or worse. I want you two to forget Malik. Do you understand?"

Both boys nodded, but Miss Shedd said, "I want to hear you say yes."

"Yes," they said. Samira could see that they were ready to leave.

But Miss Shedd was not finished.

"Good," she said. "Now we can get on to what's really important. We have three hundred children here. The children who were in the Baqubah camp know each other well, but the rest of you have come from several other camps. We all have to get along so we're going to have rules that everybody knows about. I'm going to read you a few rules that some of the children here have suggested."

They listened. No fighting. No hitting. No lying. No stealing. No calling people names. Be friendly to strangers. Be responsible about work.

When Miss Shedd was finished, Avram spoke up. "If you have rules, you have to have punishment. People who break the rules should be punished." He said it in a flat voice, as if he was reciting something he had heard many times.

Miss Shedd looked away from the children for a moment. Samira thought that she was looking at the photograph of her father.

When her attention came back to Avram she said, "I don't want to waste my time thinking about how to punish thoughtless children. We all have more important things to do." She was silent for a moment and then added, "Of course, punishment is always possible, but we won't discuss it now."

Avram almost looked disappointed.

Miss Shedd went on, "We will have rules here and each one of you will have to find the discipline to abide by them. That is your responsibility."

She stood up and went to the door and opened it.

The children filed past her silently. They didn't speak until the door closed behind them.

Avram looked around defiantly. "Is she always like that? Why can't she just punish us? It would be easier."

Samira felt a flare of anger. "Easier for you," she said. "You could get punished and then go off and break any rule and get punished again. You don't want to be responsible."

Avram stared at her for a moment. Then he turned from the group and stalked away.

For the next few days no fights broke out. No names were called. But most of the newcomers kept to their own groups. They walked to school together, played together, even managed to sign up to do chores together.

Malik stayed apart from everyone and walked alone at the back of the line. Samira looked for his skinny figure there every day. He reminded her of the days she had spent sitting on her sleeping mat in the Baqubah camp speaking to no one, thinking there could be no friends in such a place.

"He doesn't see us," she said to Maryam one day. Malik had just hurried past without speaking. "We are just a bunch of faces to him. Not separate people he might like."

"You people who were in the Baqubah camp are lucky," said Maryam. It was Sunday right after lunch, and they had time to sit on a bench and talk. The air was cold but the sun was warm on their faces.

"Lucky?" said Samira.

"You've been together for such a long time. You really know each other. The rest of us have been in many camps. Every time I got to know another girl she was moved out or I was. I never had a good friend the way you have Anna. And the boys always had to stand up for themselves among people they didn't know. None of us learned to be very friendly."

She frowned a little and then looked at Samira.

"For me, this orphanage is better than the camps. I know you now and I don't think they're going to move us. But some of the others, they just hate being here and they don't even want to try."

A few days later Samira was in her room counting dry beans into groups of ten. Miss Shuman said this would help her with multiplication.

Suddenly she heard shouting and running feet out in the hall. She went to the door and in the dim light saw a boy holding a girl by her long braids with one hand and raising the other to strike her in the face.

The girl was Shula, one of the new members of Samira's class at school. The boy was Avram.

Shula was staring at Avram with wide eyes, screaming, "Coward. Coward. Coward."

Other girls were coming out of their rooms and moving closer to the two, who seemed to freeze. Avram's hand upraised. Shula's mouth open. But she stopped screaming.

Samira called to a little girl standing near the door of the building.

"Run, Alma," she said. "Run and find Miss Shedd or a teacher."

When Avram heard Samira say, "Miss Shedd," he let go of Shula's braids and turned to run out the door.

"Stop!" Avram paused and stared at Samira, who was astonished to realize that the loud command had come from her mouth. Before she could speak again or he could move, Miss Shedd was standing in the doorway.

"Tell me what is going on here," she said in a calm voice. She looked at Avram. "To begin with, what are you doing in the girls' dormitory?"

Avram said nothing, but Shula said fiercely, "He chased me in here. I came here for safety and he followed me."

Avram glared at her. "You spoke evil of me. You insulted me."

Miss Shedd glanced at all the girls gathered in the hallway.

"Go back to your rooms," she said. "Nothing more is going to happen. Samira, you stay here."

She waited until the girls were gone. Samira knew that most of them would be standing with their ears to their doors, hoping to hear what happened next.

Miss Shedd looked at all the closed doors and smiled just a little. She knew, too.

"We will go to my office," she said. "Samira, you can come and tell me what happened."

Shula folded her arms tight across her body and walked near Miss Shedd. Avram strode a bit ahead, trying to look as if he had nothing to do with the others.

Miss Shedd shut the door of her office firmly and sat behind her desk. She did not invite the children to sit down.

"Samira," she said, "what do you know about this?"

Samira had only a little to tell, and she ended by saying, "Shula was screaming, 'Coward.' It made Avram very angry."

Miss Shedd looked at Shula. "Why did you call Avram a coward?"

"He's my cousin," said Shula. "When they shut down the Mosul camp my brother went with the men to go back to their villages. Avram was afraid to go with them. Now he acts tough with the little boys but I know that he is not brave. He is..." She broke off as Miss Shedd shook her head.

"How old are you?" she asked Avram.

"Fourteen."

"How old is Shula's brother?"

"Sixteen."

"Shula, how old are you?"

"Fourteen."

"Did you think of defying the rule that said children under sixteen must go to an orphanage to be cared for? Did you think of trying to reach your home with a group of people you did not know? You are as old as Avram."

"But I'm a girl. I couldn't do that."

"I see. For a girl there is a reason to follow rules. For a boy, no reason. Shula, your brother had to do what he did or he would have been forced into the army. It is wrong to compare Avram to your brother. And it is wrong to call anyone by a hurtful word. We do not allow that here. I hope you understand because it will never be allowed."

Shula said, "Yes, Miss Shedd."

Then Miss Shedd fixed Avram with her bright eyes.

"Shula was wrong. But you were wrong, too. Shula is the same age as you. She can make you angry. But could she defeat you in a fight?"

Avram stared at the floor. After a moment he shook his head.

"You are the stronger one and you can hold on to her and hit her. That's not even a fair fight. It's beating up on a smaller person. Avram, I said that hurtful words are not allowed. Hitting, punching and fighting are not allowed, either. Do you understand?"

Avram nodded and then he said, "Yes, Miss Shedd."

"That's good."

Miss Shedd said nothing more for several moments. Samira knew that Shula and Avram were waiting for her to tell them what punishment they would receive. But Miss Shedd looked as if she was thinking about something far away.

Finally she spoke.

"Shula, I suspect that you're worried about your brother. He set off on a dangerous journey and until you get back to your village you will hear no news of him."

Shula stared at her. "How could I go to my village? My brother went with men who know the mountains. He had a chance. I'm stuck in an orphanage with no one to help me make the journey. I'll never get there."

Miss Shedd looked from Shula to Avram and then to Samira.

"You're wrong about that. For one thing there are people here who can help you. For another you can do many things for yourself. Samira's brother pointed out to me some time ago that all of you walked to Hamadan when you had to flee from your homes. I've been thinking about that. I am sure that all of you could walk back. But it will take planning and organizing."

Samira felt almost dizzy. Ever since the day she had found the umbar, she had been waiting for Miss Shedd to say something about making the journey back to the villages. Now she wasn't sure whether she was afraid or full of hope.

Miss Shedd got up and came around her desk to stand in front of the children.

"Are you interested in going home, Shula? Are you, Avram? And Samira?"

Samira decided she was more hopeful than afraid and answered, "Yes."

Avram nodded but looked unconvinced.

Shula said, "Of course, but…"

Miss Shedd shook her head. "We'll have time later to talk about any problems you can think of. Right now, Shula, I have a job for you. I want you to make a list of all the things we will need to take with us on a long walking journey. Not food, but other supplies. Ask other people what they think. I want the list next week."

She turned to Avram. "There's a job for you, too. We'll be walking for several weeks and camping at night. We'll have a cook and a few other adults with us. I need to know what jobs you children can do to make this journey possible. Think about it, Avram. Ask your friends what they are prepared to do and make a list of all the jobs."

She went back and sat down behind her desk. "I'll see you here in one week, with your lists."

Samira waited until the other two were gone, her heart jumping in her chest. She had to ask.

"Do you mean it, Miss Shedd? Can we walk back to our homes?"

"What Benyamin said is true. You older children already made that walk so you know you can do it. But you don't want a journey like that one, again, do you?"

"No," said Samira in a low voice. "My sister and my mother — "

"Exactly," said Miss Shedd. "You had no time to get ready. You couldn't rest on the journey. Of course people died."

Samira remembered the cart loaded with food. Her father taking tools and charcoal to boil water for tea. Taking such care.

"We had our fathers and our mothers then," she burst out. "And still everything went wrong. Now we are just orphans."

"You aren't just orphans. Look at all the things you do every day for yourselves and for the younger children. And you won't be alone on the journey. I'll be with you and others will help, too."

She looked into Samira's face for what seemed a long time. "But you're right. We won't have a lot of help. Whether we can do it will depend on you and Shula and Avram and Benyamin and every single child. I believe that you can do what has to be done. After all, I've sent Shula and Avram out to start the work."

"You mean the lists?"

"Not the lists. I can make lists. No, they'll talk to their

friends. You'll talk, too. All the children will start thinking about this idea. Then, maybe, they'll be ready to do the work. Everyone will have to help." She sighed. "Really, I'm not worried about getting you children to help. There are other people who may not like the idea at all."

"What people?" asked Samira. "Who wouldn't think we should go home?"

"We want to go from Hamadan to places beyond Lake Urmieh. We can't do it unless we get permission from government officials in several places. And every single official likes to feel he is powerful and important. It will be my job to get all the permits we must have. It won't be easy."

"But you think that in the end they will let us go home?"

"If we give them no rest and show them we're ready, Samira, I think they will."

Samira left Miss Shedd's office with her head full of questions. How long would the journey take? How could they carry everything they would need? What about the little children who couldn't walk so far? How would each child get to the right village? Who would be at home to meet her and Benyamin?

Benyamin. She had to tell Benyamin.

She found him playing a game with some other boys, using sticks to hit a ball up and down the yard. When he saw her he dropped his stick and came over at once.

"Has something happened?" he asked. "You're all red in the face."

"It hasn't happened yet," she said. "But it will. At least I think it will. Miss Shedd thinks it will so it will, won't it?"

"What are you talking about? You're not making any sense."

"I'm just excited," said Samira. "Remember how you told Miss Shedd that we all walked from our villages to Hamadan? Now she says, why can't we walk back?"

Benyamin frowned. "I probably could or maybe you." He looked around the yard. "But not everyone. You know what happened before."

"Miss Shedd says it won't be the same. We'll have time to plan and we'll take everything we need with us. She says it will be different. She says we'll get home."

They sat on a bench and Samira told him about Shula and Avram's argument and Miss Shedd's astonishing announcement.

"I think she wants us to talk about it so everyone can get used to the idea. Then when she tells us more about her plans we'll be able to start getting ready right away."

"She doesn't like to waste time, does she? Well, let's start talking."

Within a day it seemed that every child had something to say about walking home.

"A lot of people died when we ran from our villages. I'm not doing it again. I'd rather stay here." That was how Maryam felt.

"We just grabbed what we could and ran," said Anna. "This time we'll be organized. Miss Shedd will see to that. And no one will be after us, trying to kill us. The war is over."

"We could still run out of food," said Samira. "Or some child might wander off and get lost. Or people could get sick. But we have to try. We have to."

Shula and Avram were making their lists. Shula talked to

everyone and made neat lists divided into categories: dishes, cooking utensils, clothing, bedding, first-aid.

Avram tore a big piece of paper from a box of school supplies that came from America and wrote a list of tasks in big letters: Packing Up. Finding Fuel. Washing Dishes. Chopping Onions.

A week passed. On the eighth morning Miss Shedd gathered the older children in the eating room.

"I know that you have all heard about my idea that we can all walk together to get you to your home villages. I can tell you now just how we will do it. The journey will have two stages. First we will walk to the city of Tabriz on the east side of Lake Urmieh. All of you come from villages in the hills and mountains west of the lake. In Tabriz there is a big orphanage where you will stay while I send someone to find a relative or friend who will take each one of you into their families. When those people are found you will make the second stage of your journey to your own village. Right now we are planning the first stage of the journey. It will take us about thirty days to walk to Tabriz. We will need food and supplies and determination."

She held up Shula's careful lists and Avram's big piece of paper.

"This is very good work," she said. "But now we have to start putting the lists to good use. How shall we do that?" She waited, but nobody said anything so she went on. "We all want our journey to be safe and not too difficult. How can each of you help make it be that way?"

"We can pack what we need and leave unnecessary things behind," said one boy at last.

"We can mend our clothes so they are strong for the walking," said a girl.

Then Avram said loudly, "Getting ready is easy but when we are traveling there will be so many jobs that must be done. We have to prepare food and load wagons and look after babies and everything. No one can do all those things. I have to know what my job is."

Miss Shedd nodded. "You are absolutely right, Avram. There are about three hundred children in this orphanage and there won't be many adults with us. I'll be there, of course. We'll have a doctor to take care of illness or injuries, and a cook who will have a wagon with all the equipment he needs to prepare our meals. Mr. Edwards will be with us for half the journey and a man from Tabriz will come for the other half. Three women will help the cook and the doctor and two men will ride out every day to find our camping place for the night and buy fresh food from the villages. But that is all. Maybe eight adults and three hundred children. Now, in your villages, who looks after the little children who can run around? Who helps the older children with their lessons and their tasks?"

"Their mothers." "Their aunts." "Their big brothers and sisters." "Maybe cousins." "Fathers." "Grandmas and grandpas."

"Yes," said Miss Shedd. "And all those people are members of the family. Some of you have brothers or sisters or cousins here in the orphanage but most of you do not. So we will make families who will look after each other on this journey."

Samira was puzzled. Make families?

Miss Shedd smiled. "These families will be different from the families you're thinking of. We'll call them caravan families because each family will travel in a group and camp together. You'll look out for the other people in your family. Each family will have at least twelve children of different ages and, of course, girls and boys. You won't have children under five in your family because they'll be riding in carriers on the backs of mules, and the women will look after them when we camp."

Miss Shedd looked around the room once more.

"I know you're wondering who will be in your caravan family. I'll let you know very soon. And don't worry. We'll have plenty of time to prepare for the journey. It's November now and I hope we can make our journey next September. That seems like a long time, but we have a lot of work to do."

Back in their room, Samira sat on her rolled-up sleeping mat and Anna paced, first around the edge of the rug and then from corner to corner. Finally she stopped in the middle and said, "I will not be in any family without you and Elias. That's final. She says that families look after each other. Well, we already do."

"We have to have Benyamin, too. And he'll want Ashur," said Samira. "We'll just tell Miss Shedd."

"Will she listen?"

"I think she will. She wants it to work as much as we do and she knows we belong together. She's just doing what she always does, telling us enough to get us thinking."

"She expects so much."

"I know. She reminds me of my Aunt Sahra. She was

always rushing to get things done and hurrying my cousins and me. My mother would take time to listen to anything I wanted to tell her but Aunt Sahra could only stop for important things. Miss Shedd is like that."

Several days later Miss Shedd asked Samira and Anna to come to her office after dinner. When they arrived, Benyamin and Ashur were already there.

"Sit down, children," she said. "I want to tell you who will be in your caravan family. The oldest ones will be the four of you. The middle ones will be Maryam, Avram, Shula and Malik."

Anna interrupted. "That Malik. He's always going off by himself. He never talks to anyone. How will he fit into any family?"

"Our families are going to be like other families," said Miss Shedd, looking at each one of them. "That means some members won't be easy to understand or get along with. I hope that by the time we set out on our journey, Malik will feel that he belongs with you."

She picked up a piece of paper with a list of names on it. "Of course Elias will be in your family and you'll have three more of the younger children. Monna, Sheran and David. If you don't know them now, you soon will. I know that you four work well together so I'm asking you to be the leaders of your family, the big sisters and big brothers. Are you willing to do this?"

They nodded.

"Good," she said. "Now I'll give you your first job. Each family must have a name. It will make it easier to talk about the families. I want you to choose a name that reminds you of home, like the Mountain Family or the Vineyard Family. You can stay here and decide on your name. I have to go and speak with some of the other children."

When she was gone they were all quiet. A name for this new family. What could it be?

At last Benyamin said, "We could be the Rooftop Family. We slept on the roofs with our families and we played on the roofs. And we watched from the roofs."

After a minute they all agreed. They would be the Rooftop Family. They would walk to Tabriz together.

THE FAMILIES were formed. But they didn't really feel like families.

As Anna said to Samira, "There are people in this family I barely know. What kind of family is that?"

"I think it's a new kind of family," said Samira. "I hope it will work."

Miss Shedd did not just hope. She had a plan.

"Families eat together and work together," she said.

The meal schedule was rearranged so that each new family gathered together for their evening meal every day. The twelve members of the Rooftop Family sat around a big bowl of stew or rice and vegetables and each person scooped a serving into their own small bowl. They had to be careful to divide the meat fairly, if there was meat, and Anna made sure that the smaller children got their proper share.

At first there were long pauses in the conversation, but Samira and Anna, as big sisters, decided to ask questions about favorite games and stories or the worst job each person had ever had to do. In just a few days talk began as soon as the family sat down.

Samira began to feel that she was getting to know this family of hers. It was different from knowing them as friends. Maryam, for instance, never tried to get a bit more than her share and often waited to serve herself last. The ravenous boys would scoop as much as they could from the bowl, so Anna began watching out for Maryam as well as for the young ones. Small Monna was so thin and ate so slowly that she worried Samira. How could she walk to Tabriz?

Elias, on the other hand, was the youngest in the family but he ate as much as he could fit in his bowl. He also took part in every discussion. He often argued with Avram, who liked to talk about all the important jobs he would do on the journey.

"I'll run ahead and help the cook get the fire going every day," Avram said one day.

"But I can run faster," said Elias. "I'll be first to get to the camp."

"The others will find you sleeping beside the road. They'll have to pick you up and carry you." And the argument went on, getting sillier and sillier.

Malik was the only member of the family who never expressed an opinion about anything.

"I know he listens to what we say," Samira said to Anna. "I can see him almost smile when Avram boasts, and he shakes his head when we go on and on about how hard the journey will be. Maybe no one has ever listened to him and he just learned to keep quiet. If we keep eating together long enough maybe he'll talk one day."

"I think that pretty soon Miss Shedd will give us more to do than just eat together," said Anna. "I've seen her going from one dormitory to another with her lists."

Then one dark February evening, just as Elias had fallen asleep, Miss Shedd came into Samira and Anna's room with a list in her hand.

"I've come to let you know that the three of you will be moving into Dormitory Four," she said in a low voice. "All of your family will be there. The boys' rooms will be at one end of the building and the girls' at the other. Elias will move in with Benyamin and one of the other boys. Monna will be sharing your room."

"Why do we have to move?" Samira asked.

"Because I want all of the members of each family to be living in one building. Of course there will be two other families in Dormitory Four." She held the piece of paper near the lantern. "It will be the Grapevine and the River families. Living in the same building with your whole family will give you a chance to get used to working things out together. And you'll have your own workroom in the dormitory. We'll be talking about that soon."

Samira looked at the bright cloth she had saved from the sewing room and hung on the wall, and at the bookshelf Anna had made from scraps of lumber.

"But we've made this room our own," she said.

"You can take everything with you," said Miss Shedd. "Be ready to carry your things to Dormitory Four tomorrow after school."

"Elias has been with us since he was practically a baby," said Anna when Miss Shedd had gone on to the next

Celia Barker Lottridge

room. "Do you think he'll be upset about leaving us?"

"He loves Benyamin so I think he'll get used to it pretty fast. And we'll be right down the hall." Samira sat down beside the sleeping boy and smoothed his hair back from his forehead. "It's a big change for us, too."

The next afternoon they packed up their things for the short move to Dormitory Four. Samira was surprised at the big pile her belongings made. It took two trips to carry it all. She had thick clothing for the winter now and quilts and a small basket filled with a notebook and pencils and some reading books from school. The little measure from the umbar and the books she and Anna had made in Baqubah were carefully stowed in the bottom of the basket.

"Remember when everything we had would fit in that skinny cardboard box?" she said to Anna.

The new room was exactly like the one they had left. As Samira pushed tacks through the bright piece of cloth and into the mud walls, she wondered why she had made any fuss at all. The big difference was that Elias was missing.

Benyamin had come to the old room as they were packing up.

"We need you to come and live with us big boys," he said to Elias.

"Can Samira and Anna come, too?"

"They can come," said Benyamin, "but they have to live in a room down the hall. We can visit them, though." And he whisked Elias away.

Anna came in with the sleeping mats.

"We're all settled," she said. "Let's go and get Monna and her things."

As they walked along the hall, the sound of boys talking and laughing made Samira remember that she had once lived in one room with her whole family. Now the Rooftop Family was under one roof.

"It's good," she decided.

By dinnertime everyone in Dormitory Four was settled. Maryam, Shula and Sheran were in the next room and the six boys in the Rooftop Family were in two rooms down at the boys' end of the hall. Malik was with Benyamin and Elias.

"Malik likes Elias. He even laughs with him sometimes," Benyamin told Samira. "Miss Shedd told me that before he had to leave home, Malik lived with his grandmother. He never went to school and he's managed to be by himself in the camps. He's just not used to being with boys his age. Elias is easier for him."

Samira hoped that Elias would remember all the times he had laughed with her. She missed him. But now she and Elias and Malik were all part of this big new family. She decided to invite both of them to a game of shooting pebbles.

One day Miss Shedd called all the big brothers and sisters together.

"I want each family to think of something to make that will be useful to us as we travel. It could be something you make especially for the journey, or maybe you can improve something we already have. When you have a plan we'll talk about whether it will work and what supplies you will need."

The Rooftop Family met in their workroom. As they talked about the journey, Samira began to have a picture in her mind of everyone in the orphanage walking across the land.

"We'll have to be properly dressed," she thought, "and we'll have to carry what we need. But how will we carry it?"

She suddenly realized that Shula was looking at her.

"Aren't you listening to me?" Shula said. "I just said that even though the mules will be carrying most of our clothes and supplies, we'll need some things with us every day. Like our lunch and a cup."

"That's it," said Samira. "We need a bag. A flat bag with a shoulder strap."

Benyamin nodded enthusiastically. "It's a good idea. The bags can be different sizes, smaller for the smaller children. But what will they be made out of?"

"Canvas," said Samira. "They made our shoe tops out of canvas. We can sew it on a sewing machine."

They began to make a list of the supplies they would need: canvas, thread, at least one sewing machine, scissors, buttons to close the bags.

When they showed their plan to Miss Shedd, she approved it at once.

"I have to see about the canvas and other sewing supplies, but I know we can get two sewing machines again and some heavy-duty scissors from the Near East Relief office. I'll give you a piece of lighter cloth so that you can make one by hand to be a pattern for the canvas ones. You have needles and thread to do that, don't you, girls?"

They did, since it was one of their jobs to sew on buttons and mend rips in the clothes of the whole Rooftop Family.

Working out a pattern for the bags took a long time

because everyone had different ideas about the best way to do it, but in the end Samira and Anna sewed a flat bag with a flap and a button to close it. The strap was wide and would go over one shoulder and across the wearer's chest.

"Do you realize that we have to make two hundred and seventy bags?" Samira said in one of the family meetings. "Luckily the littlest children won't need them but two hundred and seventy is a lot. We have to divide up the work."

They decided that the boys would cut the canvas, the younger children would fold and pin the cloth carefully so that it would be ready to sew, and the bigger girls would do most of the sewing, though Avram and Ashur wanted to do some of that, too.

"I'll teach you how to do it without sewing your fingers," Samira promised.

Other families were painting names on tin cups or reinforcing the soles of shoes. The work got the children thinking about the journey and the list of jobs Avram had made.

Anna said to Samira, "As usual we will look after the younger children."

"Yes," said Samira, "but it will take more than the two of us to look after our Rooftop little ones. Imagine trying to keep four Eliases in sight when we are walking along a road in open country. Anyway, we'll have other things to do, too."

In the end the division of responsibility turned out to be mostly common sense. The older boys would set up camp every night and pack up in the morning. Malik surprised everyone by saying that he would load and unload the mules. The older girls would look after the younger children when they were in camp. When they were walking each younger boy or girl would be the responsibility of one of the older ones. Everyone would take a turn at helping the cook.

The young ones wanted jobs, too.

"You will help with setting up camp every day," promised Samira. "We need you to unroll the sleeping mats and roll them up in the morning. But the most important thing you will do is stay with us. With all the big girls and boys. Do you promise?"

Monna, Sheran, David and Elias all nodded solemnly.

"I wonder how many times we'll say that in thirty days of walking," Anna muttered.

The Rooftop Family was falling into patterns. The girls often invited the younger boys into their rooms to play games or hear stories. The older boys checked each evening to be sure everyone was safely in their rooms before it was time to sleep. Samira could imagine them taking a walk around the camping place of the Rooftop Family, making sure everyone was there and settled for the night.

Before the younger children went to bed, she and Anna told them stories about setting out for a long walk with all of their friends, eating lunch along the road, getting tired but singing songs to keep going and arriving at a good camping place at the end of the day to rest and eat. The story had adventures, too, but never soldiers, never people who disappeared or were hungry or sick.

Most nights Samira lay under her quilt with the journey filling her head. She tried to put herself to sleep by remembering the careful plans for food and water and rest and by thinking about how the people in the Rooftop Family would look out for each other and how Miss Shedd would watch over everything.

But sometimes as she fell asleep her mind filled with the rhythm of walking, walking with no rest. She would wake suddenly, sure that someone was missing.

Was it Mama? No, Mama didn't belong in this dim room. Small Monna was beside her. And Anna. Elias? He was down the hall with Benyamin.

They were all there. In Hamadan. Waiting to go home.

WINTER PASSED. Spring passed. Even summer passed. The umbar was crammed with supplies for the journey. Samira and Anna looked at the Rooftop Family's clothes and went to see Miss Shedd.

"It looks as if we might have to travel in cold weather, but we don't all have warm jackets that fit us," Samira told her.

"And some of us can't squeeze our feet into our extra-strong shoes anymore," said Anna. "Our feet have grown."

"We'll make more jackets and shoes," said Miss Shedd. "If only we could make the letters of permission we're waiting for."

September passed and the letters did not come.

"Do you think a person can die of having to wait and wait and wait?" asked Anna,

"I don't think so," said Samira. "We've been waiting to go home for years already."

Then, on an ordinary October morning, Miss Shedd came into the eating room in the middle of breakfast. All chatter stopped.

"Children," she said. "I have good news. The letters of permission are on their way. We should be able to set out on our journey in three days. There will be no more school after tomorrow because you'll be busy with preparations."

On the last day of school Samira looked at the big map of Persia that hung on the wall. It was easy to find Hamadan, midway between Baghdad and Tehran. Up in the left-hand corner, near the top of the map, was Lake Urmieh with the city of Tabriz just above it. She found the city of Urmieh, too, but Ayna and the other villages she could remember were not named.

She studied the space on the map between Hamadan and Tabriz. She saw many wavy lines that meant mountains, and empty spaces with few towns marked.

So much to get across.

Miss Shuman came and looked at the map with her.

"I know that you children can make this journey. You just have to keep going and take care of each other. You may even have a good time." She turned around and spoke to all the girls. "I know I'll hear news of you when you get to Tabriz. I wish you safe traveling."

That was one day. Now another day had passed. Piles of bedding, a bundle of clothing for each child, baskets of spoons and bowls were lined up in the yard ready to be loaded onto mules or into wagons. The umbar had been emptied of dried fruits and vegetables, rice and flour. Miss Shedd was walking among the piles one last time, checking lists, making sure that nothing was forgotten.

The children, too, went over their clothes and belongings again and again. Each was equipped with a canvas bag made by the Rooftop Family, and in each bag was a cotton scarf in case of dust storms, a drinking cup, a washcloth and any small things too precious to be left behind. Samira managed to squeeze her two books and the little measure she had found in the umbar into her bag. Then she had to persuade Elias that his stone collection would be too heavy to carry.

"There will be plenty of stones along the way, I promise you," she told him. He nodded, but she saw him slip three special round stones that always hit their mark into his pocket.

She went to find Hanna, who had come from the city to help the younger children get ready. Hanna was worried about the weather.

"I know you have your warm jackets," she said to Samira. "But you'll still be on the road in November. Cold weather will come. Wind and rain and even snow. And you children sleeping on the ground." She shook her head.

"But we have to go," said Samira. "After all this waiting."

"I know. You have to go when you have the chance." She smiled. "And you have Susan Shedd. She won't listen if you complain about wind or snow, but she'll get you there." She gave Samira a hug before she went back to the city.

Mules and their chavadars — the men who would load them and drive them all the way to Tabriz — had arrived that morning and were waiting restlessly outside the gate along with three big wagons called furgoons. The furgoons had canvas tops for shelter from rain and sun. One would be a kitchen wagon and one the doctor's wagon. The third would carry supplies.

The orphans who were too small to walk would ride two by two in wooden carriers fastened on either side of a mule's saddle. Each carrier was like a box with a wooden seat inside.

Celia Barker Lottridge

Monna got tired very easily so she would ride in a carrier though she was almost six. This plan worried Elias, who was younger than Monna.

"I will walk," he stated firmly.

"You just turned five and some five-year-olds will be riding," Samira told him. "Do you feel big enough to walk with us? It will be a long way every day and we can't carry you. You're too heavy."

"I'm big and I'm strong," Elias said. "I can run faster than you." He raced to the farthest end of the yard to prove it.

There was no point arguing, and Samira knew that if Elias couldn't manage the walk there would be room for him on one of the mules.

Besides the mules there were horses for the outriders who would go ahead of the caravan and find camping places, buy eggs and meat, and ask village women if they could bake bread for three hundred people. Miss Shedd would have a horse, too. A big black horse named Sumbul.

"You children will be strung out in a very long line," Miss Shedd explained. "On Sumbul I can ride up and down the line and make sure that all is well."

During the evening meal on the third day Miss Shedd came into the eating room.

"Something's wrong," said Benyamin.

Miss Shedd waited for the children to stop talking. Then she said, "I'm sorry to tell you that we won't start out tomorrow. The general in charge of military affairs here in Hamadan says that he has no orders from the Minister of War so he won't let us leave. There's nothing we can do but wait until they get their orders straight. Lots of games and circle dances will help pass the time tomorrow. Maybe I'll come and join you."

But she didn't. She went down into the city to talk to the people in the Near East Relief office. But day after day passed with no news. The orphans kept on waiting.

The warm weather of autumn was coming to an end. Nights were chilly, and Samira could feel the edge of frost in the air. Miss Shedd had wanted to set out in September when the harvest was coming in and the caravan could buy grapes and melons and squash from villagers. But now it was October.

"We have good shoes and warm jackets," she said to Anna. "We can make it, can't we?"

"If we leave today we can," said Anna. "But we're not leaving today." She was busy with the three- and four-year-olds and didn't want to waste her time thinking about what might happen next.

Samira went to talk to Benyamin. She found him squatting on the ground playing a game with two other boys. Malik stood a little distance away, watching. The players held small stones in their hands and on a count of three each boy threw several pebbles on the ground. The one who threw the largest number won, but only if his number was only one higher than the next one down. Often no one won for a long time, but that just kept the boys playing.

Suddenly a picture came into Samira's mind, a picture of Benyamin and his friends playing this game in Ayna. She was watching them from the rooftop so she could only see the tops of their heads and their hands reaching out to throw down the pebbles.

Those boys. Where were they now?

Benyamin stood up and came over to Samira. After a moment Malik squatted down with the other boys and picked up the rocks.

Samira could feel herself smiling, and Benyamin said, "Are we going? Have you heard something?"

"No. There's no news. I was smiling about Malik. He's willing to be part of our caravan family now, just like the rest of us. But, Benyamin, if we get to Ayna we might find no family at all. I'm not sure I want to go."

"All this waiting is giving us too much time to think and we don't know anything about how things are in Ayna. We have to get to Tabriz and see what happens next."

It was true, Samira knew. It was impossible to stay in this place now, anyway. The whole orphanage had been packed away. It was as empty as it had been when they arrived more than a year ago.

"Yes," she said. "We have to go."

When she got back to the schoolyard she found Miss Shedd waving a piece of paper above her head.

"Get everyone," she called out.

In minutes the yard was filled with children. Miss Shedd stood on one of the packing cases and spoke in a loud, clear voice.

"This letter says that our final letter of permission will be delivered by a messenger early tomorrow. We'll gather here right after breakfast, ready for the journey."

She stretched her arms wide, as if she wanted to reach out to all the children. "I hope you have been happy in the Hamadan Orphanage," she said. "I have been happy to be here with you but it is time to give you a chance to get out from behind these walls and get on with your lives."

She jumped off the crate and made her way through the crowd of children. There was a moment of silence and then everyone began to talk.

Samira and Anna gathered Elias and Sheran and Monna and David in their room.

"You heard Miss Shedd, didn't you?" asked Samira. The children nodded. "So you know that tomorrow we will start our journey." Again they all nodded.

"Tell us what you will do tomorrow," said Anna.

The answers tumbled out. "We'll stay near you." "We'll remember our bags." "We'll walk but no running."

"And if you forget, who will you ask?"

"You or you or Benyamin or Ashur."

Then Monna spoke. "We'll come back here after, won't we?"

Samira looked around the bare room. Nothing was left in it except the things that would go with them tomorrow. But it was home. How could it be that they would never come back?

"We won't come back here," she said. "But we're going to find new places to live. New homes. And we're all making the journey together."

That night all of the girls had a hard time settling down. Each one packed and repacked her bag until Anna said, "That's enough. Everyone into bed."

In a few minutes the girls' rooms were quiet, but Samira knew that Anna was still awake.

"Remember Mrs. McDowell?" she whispered.

"Yes, of course I do."

"She would say that this is a step in the right direction."

"An awful lot of steps," answered Anna, and suddenly she giggled. "I know that Mrs. McDowell never dreamed we would have to walk home. I don't think she would choose to make this journey. She loved transport."

A memory from home slid into Samira's mind. The whole family walking with Papa down the road and around a few bends to get him started on his journey to the market in the city.

"Come with me and pour me on my way," he would say. That's what people in the village always said when they traveled away from home. "Come with me and pour me on my way."

"Mrs. McDowell would pour us on our way," she whispered.

Anna stopped giggling and said, "Yes, she would."

FOUR

A Long Way to Go

The Journey
October 1923

SAMIRA woke at the first light of the gray dawn and saw that Anna was already dressed and rolling up her sleeping mat.

"I'll get the other girls up," she said to Samira. "You can roll up the rest of the mats."

The day had begun. They found the boys out in the yard, waiting for breakfast. The eating room was closed so they sat on the ground to eat their bread and drink their tea. Then they ran to get their sleeping mats and quilts. Benyamin and Ashur took them out through the gate to the chavadar who was to carry their things. They helped him load the mules and came back to the yard where everyone was waiting.

Miss Shedd was standing near the gate, ready to receive the final letter of permission that would allow them to leave Hamadan. She was wearing trousers and a jacket, and she carried a small whip under her arm.

"Why does she have that whip?" asked Anna.

Benyamin answered, "A horse sometimes needs a touch of the whip. Anyway, she's riding like a man, not a fine lady, so she has to have what a man would have."

Samira thought he was right. Miss Shedd could not look like a weak woman. Not on this journey.

For a long time the children sat on the ground, waiting

quietly. Then the small ones began to get restless, and Miss Shedd came around to the families and said, "I don't know when the wretched official is going to appear. You had better get some games going."

So Anna and Samira organized some circle games. Most of the older children wandered around chatting aimlessly until one of the teachers got them running races instead. Malik stood leaning against the nearest building, not moving, but Samira could see that he was keeping track of every member of the Rooftop Family.

Then it was lunchtime.

The cook came around with packets of lunch he had ready for them.

"This is your first meal of the journey. Next time you'll be carrying your lunch in those fancy sacks you folks made."

The packets contained bread and cheese and dried fruit. No one was very hungry but eating passed the time. After lunch some of the younger children simply fell asleep on the ground and the rest just sat. Waiting.

Then, suddenly, there was the sound of a horse galloping up the slope. A man in a uniform with gold braid at his cuffs came riding through the gate. He dismounted and handed a big envelope to Miss Shedd. She took a moment to speak with him. Then she opened the envelope and took out a piece of paper.

As she read it the expression on her face changed from relief and joy to disappointment and anger. Samira could see it quite plainly. What had happened?

For several minutes Miss Shedd spoke with the messenger. Then she gathered around her the doctor, the cook, the outriders and Mr. Edwards. They talked with their heads close together. The children waited for what seemed a very long time.

At last Miss Shedd went and got a wooden box.

"She's going to tell us what has gone wrong this time," said Anna in a gloomy voice.

"Shhh," said Samira. "Listen."

Miss Shedd stepped up on the box and looked out at the children.

"We have a serious problem," she said. "Three hundred and ten of us are ready tó set out on our journey but the government has chosen to give permission for only two hundred and eighty to leave today. This official will be counting and he will not let any more go out of the gate. We have decided that the two oldest boys in each family will stay here for now. As soon as their permit comes they will join us."

Samira looked around. Miss Shedd could not have said those words. But everyone was looking stunned. They had all heard her.

Miss Shedd saw their dismay. "I know that asking these big brothers to stay here so that the rest of us can go is hard for everyone. It's hard for me, too. But there is no time to weep and argue. This permit is for today. Tomorrow they might decide not to let any of us go. Say goodbye to the boys for just a few days. Then wake up the young ones and follow our plan."

Miss Shedd stepped down from the box. She went to her horse, put her foot in the stirrup and swung herself into the saddle.

Samira went over to Benyamin.

"I can't leave you here," she said. "I won't. We have to stay together. Anyway, how can we manage without you and Ashur?"

Benyamin looked taller all of a sudden. "Samira, Miss Shedd is right. You have to go. For the next few days you and Anna can look after our family. Everyone will help. That's why we're a family, so that there is always someone to step in and take care of things." He gave her a quick hug. "Ashur and I will help you get organized now."

Indeed, everyone needed to be organized. Some young children were crying because they were wakened so suddenly. Others were wandering around looking confused. All over the yard children were wailing and calling to each other.

Benyamin went up to Malik.

"Malik," he said. "For a few days you and Avram will be the oldest brothers in the Rooftop Family. The rest of the family is going to need you to be with them and help them. Will you do it?"

Malik didn't say anything for a minute, and in the hubbub Samira was afraid he would never answer. But he finally looked at Benyamin and said, "Well, if they listen to me I will."

"That's all I need to hear. Now let's get going."

Samira counted heads. "Two little girls. Two little boys. Malik, Avram, Shula, Anna, Maryam and me. Ten of us. Do you all have your bags?"

Everyone nodded.

"All right, Rooftop Family," said Ashur. "Benyamin and I

will walk with you to the gate. Remember, all of you, look for Samira or Anna or Malik or Avram when you need help. Stay together. Remember to — "

"We have to let them go," said Benyamin. "They'll manage."

Then the gate was in front of them. It was open just enough for one child at a time to go through. The official tapped each child on the head with his pen, counting them as they went past.

When the Rooftop Family was outside the wall Samira turned to take a last look at Benyamin, but there were so many people crowding around the gate that she couldn't see him.

She reached out for Monna. There wasn't time to find the mule carrying the box she should be riding in. She would have to walk this first part of the journey.

They all turned to go down the slope, away from the orphanage and away from the city.

Elias came to her and said, "Why are you crying?"

Samira put her hand to her cheek. Tears were running down her face.

"I'm not sure. We're going home at last but this time we're leaving things behind, too." The room in the dormitory. The umbar. Miss Shuman. Benyamin.

She managed a smile for Elias.

"I won't cry anymore," she said. "We have to walk."

They walked. The sun set behind the mountains and they were still walking. Monna began to droop, and Samira and Anna took turns carrying her. Elias stumbled but he insisted that he could keep walking. Samira was tired, too, but comforted to see that all the children in the Rooftop Family were together with Malik always on the outside of the group, always nearby.

When it was nearly dark Miss Shedd came by on Sumbul. She dismounted and led him as she walked beside Samira and Anna.

"We won't go much farther," she said. "It's too late to camp properly but luckily it's not going to rain. We'll see that you all get sleeping mats and quilts and food. I know it's hard without the boys, but we're doing fine." She got back on her horse and went on to the next group.

By the time they stopped it was very dark. There was no moon and clouds covered the stars. Samira knew that somewhere out there two hundred and seventy children were trying to find the places were they should sleep. She was glad she only had to think about the ten in her family.

She was so worn out that she didn't care whether the mat she lay down on and the quilt she pulled over her were hers. She just lay there, not even feeling hungry, but when someone came and put raisins and a piece of cheese in her hand, she ate them and felt a little better. She fell asleep knowing that the Rooftop Family was around her in the darkness.

In the morning Miss Shedd came around just as Samira was waking up.

"I'm making sure that everyone is here," she said. "It was such a rush yesterday that a few people fell asleep before they found their families. But no one is missing."

"Malik made sure no one wandered or got left behind," Samira told her. "He was always watching."

Miss Shedd looked at the lumps of quilt that were all that

could be seen of most of the children. She located one of the bigger lumps and walked over to it.

"I see that you're awake, Malik," she said. "You did a good job of keeping your family together yesterday. Now, do you know which chavadar has the Rooftop Family's supplies?"

Malik sat up. "Yes, Miss Shedd. I'm in charge of loading and unloading."

"Good. Go and talk to him now. Make sure he knows who you are. Nobody got the right bedding last night so you'll have to get that sorted out. And, Malik, ask others in your family to give you the help you need."

As Malik went off, Samira thought he was probably more scared of asking the family for help than of talking to a strange chavadar.

She stood up and looked around. Now she could see what nearly three hundred children looked like scattered around a bare pasture. Most were still asleep but a few were sitting up and stretching or standing and shaking themselves to straighten their clothes. Last night they had simply lain down in what they were wearing so now there was no need to get dressed.

She could see steaming basins of hot water set up by the doctor's wagon ready for children to wash their faces and hands. The privies were farther off.

There was a big samovar sitting on the table folded out from the cook wagon. A samovar meant tea, and Samira suddenly wanted tea very, very much. Hot tea. She took her cup out of her bag and went to stand in the line of children waiting for breakfast.

While she waited she looked beyond the camp. Empty

land and mountains stretched in one direction, and she could see the wide dirt road they would travel that day. In the other direction was the Hamadan Orphanage. She couldn't see it but it had to be there because Benyamin was there, waiting to join them.

She took her tea and some bread spread with stewed apricots back to where the Rooftop Family had been sleeping. The younger children were awake with their quilts pulled up to their chins. They were waiting for her to tell them what to do.

"You can all get up," she said. "Monna, give that Anna a little poke. She's the only lazybones here."

Anna snorted. "I'm awake. I just don't want to open my eyes and see where I am." She sat up. "You're already drinking tea. That's not fair!"

"It's a little reward for waking up early," said Samira. "But it's Malik who really deserves a reward. He's already gone to meet our chavadar. He'll make sure that we have our own things tonight." She looked around and saw Malik making his way through the children and sleeping mats scattered around the field.

He looked at the Rooftop Family and said clearly, "Time to get up!"

Everyone stared at him. None of them had ever heard Malik speak so loudly before. He went on more quietly, "Well, it is. We have a long way to walk today. That's what Miss Shedd told me." He stopped and looked at the ground.

"Malik is right," said Anna, and she scrambled up and shook out her skirt. "I hope I won't have to sleep in my skirt again. Too lumpy and look at it now."

"We're all just the same," said Maryam. "I'm hungry." She walked off toward the cook wagon and came back a few minutes later with a stack of bread and apricots for everyone.

"Mr. Edwards will come around with tea. Get out your cups and he'll fill them," she said.

"After you've eaten take the cloth that's in your bag and wash your face," said Samira. "Anna and I will brush your hair if you need help."

"And you'd better hurry," said Anna. "Malik's rolling up the mats and quilts. We'll be starting soon."

Samira helped Malik carry the bedding to the place where the mules were tethered. The bedding they had used had green tags. This meant it really belonged to the Mountain Family, so they found the chavadar in charge of supplies for that family.

He looked at Malik and said, "You'd better give me a hand loading up."

Malik went over to one of the mules, and Samira heard him talking as he tied bundles to its saddle.

"It's not going to be so bad. You're strong. You can carry this load. It'll be easy." The mule twitched its ears and seemed to be listening.

Samira felt as if she was eavesdropping on a conversation between friends, so she went back to the family.

She said to Anna, "Malik talks to the mules and they listen. I think he said more to a mule in just a few minutes than I've heard him say to people in a year."

Anna wasn't paying much attention. She was checking to be sure that the younger children had packed their bags carefully and that the wet washing cloths were tied to the strap to dry.

Miss Shedd came riding by. "Everyone up and ready to start, please. Don't leave anything behind. Remember the order of travel."

Samira remembered. The outriders had left before anyone else was awake. They would go ahead and find a camping place and maybe a village where they could buy fresh bread.

After today the three wagons would also leave early. That way the cook would have time to warm up the food he had cooked the night before and have it hot when the children arrived at the camping place. He would leave behind breakfast bread and fruit and a packet of lunch for each child.

The walking children would start out next, each family taking its place in the line. The Rooftop Family traveled between the Mountain Family and the Sun Family. The Sun Family would lead today. Tomorrow the Rooftop Family would go first. The day after that they would move to the back of the line of children. Miss Shedd had explained that this way each family would have at least one turn at setting the pace for the whole caravan.

The mules carrying the bundles would come after the children, and last of all the mules carrying the small children with Mr. Edwards to look after them.

Samira had heard Miss Shedd explaining this plan to Mr. Edwards.

"We'll let the walkers get well ahead before the mules start. If the walking children see the mules they might want to ride, too. It's better that they don't even see them."

As the Rooftop Family set out, Samira looked back. She could see the long line of children walking. But the big boys were not there.

What was Benyamin doing right now? How had the night been for him?

She turned to Anna who was walking just behind her.

"We took all the bedding with us. How did the boys sleep last night at the orphanage with no quilts? It's cold there, too."

"Don't worry about those boys," said Anna. "They have the teachers and Near East Relief people to look after them. We have to be thinking about the children right here. They're going to get tired pretty soon."

It was true. Before long some of the children were dragging their feet and beginning to grumble. At least they were staying in a group and not straying off the road. That was mostly because Malik would run down one side of the group and up the other, keeping everyone on the road. Would he be able to keep it up all day?

Samira began to sing a song everyone knew. Some joined in and they all walked a little faster to the rhythm of the music. As they rounded a curve she looked at the road ahead of them. It was downhill now but she knew it would be uphill before long.

Suddenly she remembered the road over the high pass from Kermanshah. They had made a steep climb then. They could climb another mountain now.

When the sun was high in the sky they stopped for a rest. Miss Shedd came by on Sumbul.

"I went ahead to check on the place the outriders have

found for our camp tonight. It's a threshing floor near a village. It's nice and flat and the village women are baking bread for us. So we have fresh bread to look forward to. We'll be there in time for rest and games."

Samira wanted to ask for news of the boys but she knew that was silly. What could Miss Shedd know? So she said nothing.

The day was still bright when they got to the camping place, but all the younger children just sat down on the ground. They were too tired for games so Anna and Maryam settled down to tell them stories. Everyone else had jobs to do, too. It was Shula and Avram's turn to help the cook, and Samira and Malik went to get the family's clothes and bedding.

The chavadar who had the Rooftop Family's supplies scowled at Samira and spoke only to Malik. Even when Samira asked him whether she could take some things out of the bundles instead of taking the whole bundle, he answered by speaking to Malik.

"You open the bundles. She should take what she wants and go. But you have to help me tie them up again."

Samira thought, "He wishes I wasn't here at all but he'll have to get used to it. I'm going to help Malik whether this man likes it or not."

She quickly found socks so that all the children could wash their feet and wear clean socks to bed. She also found the long sleeping shirts. Tonight the children could take off their shirts and trousers and skirts and sleep more comfortably.

Dinner was hot soup made of lentils and onions, along with fresh rounds of bread baked in the nearby village. After the Rooftop Family's bowls were washed, Samira and Maryam took them to the cook wagon. The cook was busy filling baskets with bread and dried apricots for breakfast the next day.

"We're putting the samovar in the supply wagon so that you can have hot tea for breakfast. And you can take lunch for tomorrow away with you now. Hand it out to your brothers and sisters." He gave them a sack of hard-boiled eggs, some dates and some bread that was dry and crisp.

"What about dinner tomorrow?" asked Maryam. "Do you have that ready, too?"

"It will be on the fire tonight," said the cook. "Lamb stew with yellow peas and rice. Tomorrow night it will be good and hot when you all come trailing in."

SAMIRA needed the thought of that stew as she trudged along the dusty road the next morning. The Rooftop Family was first in line, so they had to set a brisk pace for everyone following.

"I keep thinking that it must be almost time to stop for the night," said Shula as she walked beside Samira. "Then I remember that we haven't even had lunch yet. And we have to get all the way to Tabriz. Do you think we can make it?"

"We have to forget about Tabriz," said Samira. "It's too far away to think about. I do believe we'll get to the next camping place. That's enough for now."

When they did arrive at the camping place the cook wagon was there as planned, but before anyone could have supper the beds had to be laid out and any blistered feet or upset stomachs seen to by the doctor.

Anna went to collect Monna as soon as the small children came in on the mules.

"I was worried that she wouldn't be safe with those mules," Anna told Samira when they came back. "But there's no way she can fall out of the carrier. I'm going to make her a little cushion out of a couple of extra washing cloths. I think it's a pretty bumpy ride."

Monna didn't complain about the bumps.

"I could see all around," she said, "but I didn't have anyone to talk to." She hurried over to Sheran and David and Elias who were lying flat on the ground, resting. For once she had more energy than even Elias. She sat down and began to toss a ball from hand to hand — a very special ball she had made out of cloth and stuffed with sawdust. Elias watched the ball and soon said, "Throw it to me," and in a minute the four of them were playing a game.

That night Samira lay on her back looking at the stars. They made the same patterns her father had pointed out to her from the roof of the house in Ayna. She thought of Benyamin. He could be on the road looking at the stars, too. Or maybe he was still stuck behind the walls of the orphanage.

At least the weather was calm and clear. The boys should be able to travel fast.

The calm weather lasted a few more days. Then a strong wind came sweeping across the open land and blew dust into every fold of cloth and skin. If Samira opened her mouth to say a word she could feel grit between her teeth. She wrapped her scarf over her mouth and nose and trudged along with her head down, trying to see through squinted eyes. There was a lot of stumbling and complaining.

Only Malik said nothing as he moved among the children of the Rooftop Family, touching any stragglers on the shoulder to lead them back to the group.

By the time they stopped to eat at midday, the wind had died down, and Samira used her first drink of water to rinse the dust from her mouth.

Malik came and sat near her, and she decided to ask him a question.

"Are you counting us as we walk, Malik?"

For a long time Malik just chewed his bread. Then he said, "I don't exactly count. I just know how many should be there. It's like sheep."

"Sheep," said Samira, feeling foolish.

"You know. When you have a flock to look after you just know how many big ones are there and how many small ones. It's like a pattern. If a piece is missing, you know."

"Your father had sheep?" said Samira.

"Not my father. The village. I took the village sheep up to the hills. My father was... gone." Malik shut his mouth in a way that told Samira he would say no more.

She said, "Would you like some of my raisins?" He held out his hand and took them.

"Thank you," he said. Then he got up and walked away.

Samira watched him go. As he walked she could see him casting his eyes over the group of children, checking to see that they were there, but not stopping to speak or smile.

Where had his father gone? Maybe he was dead. But then Malik would surely have said, "My father died."

Suddenly she remembered a boy in Ayna. A boy whose father was never named. His mother looked after him but she seldom came out of her house. The boy had a donkey. He would help bring the harvest in from the fields or take a load of melons or grapes to another village. Sometimes she would see him walking through Ayna, talking to his donkey.

What had happened to that boy when the whole village ran away from danger? She would never know.

That night they put up the tents to shelter them in case the wind came up again. Everyone struggled with canvas and poles, and Samira thought of Benyamin as she pounded fiercely at a peg with a heavy rock, trying to force it into the hard ground.

Miss Shedd suddenly appeared with a big mallet in her hand.

"I'll do that," she said.

She gave the peg several whacks, then straightened up and rubbed her back for a moment.

"I was counting on those big boys to take charge of a lot of this sort of work. But the rest of us will learn how to do it. When they finally arrive, the boys will find we can do everything ourselves and they can just laze around."

She looked up at the sky. It was full of clouds, moving fast.

"I almost hope it rains. That would settle the dust. The doctor will be around to check on everyone's eyes. The dust can cause problems."

She gave the peg one more whack that drove it in and went on to another tent.

The next day there was no wind and the sun shone, but the children were tired and their eyes were still sore. They wanted to stop and rest much more often than Miss Shedd would allow.

In the middle of the afternoon the Rooftop Family came across a boy lying in a ditch beside the road. He seemed to be asleep.

Samira poked him gently in the shoulder with her foot.

"What are you doing?" she said. "Don't you belong to the Vineyard Family? They're up ahead of us."

"I'm resting," said the boy. "I'll get up and come along when most of the line has passed."

The boy was not very big, and Anna reached down and lifted him up by the shoulders.

"You'd better get up and walk now," she said. "You're practically asleep and you might wake up and find yourself all alone. Would you like that?"

The boy shook his head. "But I'm tired. Why won't Miss Shedd let us stop and rest?"

"We have a long way to go and winter is coming. That's what she'd say if you asked her," said Anna.

"I don't want to hear about it," said the boy. But he walked off to find his family.

Samira knew that Miss Shedd was right. They had to keep walking even though it was hard.

A few days later she said to Anna, "Every day I can walk a little faster and I think we go a little farther. Sometimes I even worry that Benyamin and the other boys will never catch us. We've been gone for ten days and we don't know if they've even left Hamadan."

"They'll catch up with us," said Anna.

The country they were walking through was changing. The road was rising slowly, up and up. One day Samira found herself thinking that she didn't care about getting to Tabriz.

She just wanted to stop walking. Going up this road was harder than it should have been, but she didn't know why.

That night they stopped in a caravanserai. It had been built in the days when camel caravans had traveled this road and needed places to stop for the night. There was a big walled yard and stables for animals. On one side of the yard were low buildings with small rooms where travelers used to sleep. Now their roofs were falling in.

The Rooftop Family found a corner where the walls offered shelter from the wind. They quickly arranged their sleeping mats on the ground. They ate lentil stew and had just crawled under their quilts when Miss Shedd came by to see that everyone was settled for the night.

She looked around at the old walls.

"Thousands of people have slept here over the years. Before the war these buildings would have sheltered people traveling between Turkey and Hamadan and farther east."

Turkey.

"Miss Shedd," Samira called. "Are we on the road to Turkey now?"

"Yes. If we kept on over the mountains we would get to the city of Urmieh. But in a few days we'll turn north and take the road to Tabriz."

"I knew I remembered," Samira said, almost to herself. "We took this road when we came down from Ayna. I have been here before."

She wondered why she hadn't seen this caravanserai when she came past on that other journey. It seemed so big now. But then she was not seeing the things around her. Only the road. Only the other frightened people.

"Will we go to Sain Kala?" she asked.

"You remember Sain Kala? It's just a village. But, yes, we'll be near Sain Kala. We'll stop at the river and you children can go swimming. I want to spend a little time there myself. After Sain Kala we'll turn toward Tabriz. That will be in two or three days. Now, go to sleep."

She stood there for a few minutes. Samira could see her dark shape, tall against the starry sky. She closed her eyes so that she wouldn't see Miss Shedd move away.

The next day word spread among the older children that they were walking on the same road most of them had taken when they fled from the war. How it spread Samira wasn't sure, because no one talked much. They were very quiet that day, each person remembering or trying not to remember.

In the middle of the morning Malik hurried up to her and said, "Shula is sitting in the road back there. She's crying."

Samira found Shula crouched with her hands over her face, wailing, "My mother. My mother."

The younger children gathered around her, their eyes wide and worried. Anna appeared and said quickly, "See if you can calm her, Samira. I'll take these children and go on. Malik, Avram must have gone on ahead. Find him."

Samira knelt down beside Shula. "Come. Move out of the road. We must let the others pass."

Shula rose with tears streaming down her face and let Samira lead her to a patch of grass. There she sank down and sobbed, "My mother died along this road. Leave me so I will die here, too. The journey is too hard. I can't go on."

Samira didn't know what to say. What Shula said was true. Her mother had died and the journey was hard.

She sat down and put her arm around Shula's shoulders.

"We could sit here thinking of our mothers and cry together," she thought. "But if I cry, how will I stop? I don't want to stay here crying."

"Shula. Why have you stopped walking?" It was Miss Shedd's voice, not unkind but wanting an answer.

Samira stood up. Avram was standing nearby looking helpless.

"Shula is remembering her mother who died on this road. She wants to give up. This journey is too hard for her, she says."

Miss Shedd sat down on the ground. She took Shula's hands away from her face and looked at her for a long time.

"Shula," she said. "This journey is not easy but it is not dangerous, not at all like that other journey. When you think of your mother remember how glad she would be to know you are going home. You may be sad but you must think of the other children. They need you to be with them."

She lifted Shula to her feet and guided her back to the road.

"Go and walk with your family," she said. "Sitting by the road wailing will do you no good." She looked at Samira. "I'll come back soon and see how you're doing."

She strode off and Samira saw that her horse was waiting for her.

Shula was still sniffling but she didn't sit down and wail again. She looked at Samira and said, "She didn't even say I was right to cry for my mother. She doesn't know how we suffered."

"No," said Samira. "She doesn't. But she knows that if we don't go home we might always be sad. That's why she is taking us on this journey. She's trying to take us home."

When the travelers finally stopped for the night it was raining, but the outriders had found dry stables for everyone to sleep in. The women of the village had swept the stable floors and brought enough fuel to make a fire where the children could take turns warming themselves.

The fire and the smell of the stew in big iron pots seemed to reach out to the ones who had been remembering the last time they had walked this road. They sat down together without talking. The little children who remembered nothing of that journey ran up and down the long stables shouting until it was time to eat.

Mr. Edwards came and stood beside the fire.

"Children," he said. "Friends. I have to say goodbye. Tomorrow very early I will begin riding back to Hamadan. In a day or two Mr. Shields from Tabriz will join you and take my place for the rest of the journey. You are on a great adventure and I'm glad I could come with you part of the way. I wish you well as you travel home."

The children crowded around him to say goodbye.

When Samira had her turn she said, "I wish you were coming all the way, Mr. Edwards. We have known you so long."

"Since the fields of Kermanshah," said Mr. Edwards. "Happy traveling, Samira."

When the girls were going to bed, Anna said to Samira, "You know why Mr. Edwards came on this trip instead of Miss Shulman, don't you?"

"Why?" said Samira.

"Because he's a man. Miss Shedd takes care of everything but there has to be a man to talk to some people."

Samira thought of the chavadar who treated her as if she was invisible. He would only talk to Malik.

"Yes," she said. "You're right."

THE NEXT morning Samira went with Malik as she always did to help him carry the bedding to the chavadar. They were just coming into the area where the mules were stabled when they heard a loud and angry voice. The chavadar who looked after the Rooftop Family's mules was shouting at Miss Shedd and shaking his fist.

Miss Shedd was listening. Sumbul stood beside her. He was listening, too, and his ears twitched nervously.

The man was shouting in Persian so Samira couldn't understand what he was saying. She knew that Miss Shedd didn't speak very much Persian, but she was standing as if she was planted in that spot and would not move until the man was quiet.

The chavadar shouted louder. He held out his hand and rubbed his thumb against his fingers. Then he said some words in Syriac.

"He wants her to pay him more money," Samira whispered to Malik.

Malik nodded. His eyes were fixed on the chavadar, and Samira knew that skinny and young as he was, he was ready to leap on the man. She put her hand on his shoulder.

Miss Shedd was shaking her head vigorously. She said no in Syriac in a low, firm voice.

The man leaned toward her and gestured to the mules and shook his head. If she didn't give him more money his mules weren't going anywhere.

Miss Shedd just stared at him. He took a small step toward her and put his hand on the dagger that was stuck in his belt.

Suddenly, without turning, Miss Shedd reached over to Sumbul and pulled her little whip out of its loop in the harness. She said no again, a little louder, and lifted the whip. Its lash whipped through the air but the man jumped back and it did not touch him.

He looked at Miss Shedd for a moment, then turned, spat on the ground and walked away.

Miss Shedd watched him go. Then she put the whip back in its loop and patted Sumbul's neck.

"Thank you for standing by me, old friend," she said. She turned to Samira and Malik. "And thank you for keeping still. I know you wanted to help but I had to deal with that man. He's been paid. They've all been paid the whole amount we agreed on. But he thought he could get more while I was on my own with no man to back me up. We have no money to spare, of course. We have to buy food and fuel from the village people with what little we have. And anyway, I would not let him push me around just because he thought he could."

She looked beyond Samira and Malik toward the road.

"I won't be stopped from getting you children home. You can believe that." She went over to Sumbul and put her foot in the stirrup. With one motion she was on the horse, looking down at them.

"Well, that was an invigorating start to the day, wasn't it?" she said. "Now it's time for us to be on our way." She clicked her tongue and Sumbul walked briskly out of the camp as if he, too, wanted to leave this place.

Later as they tramped along the road, Samira told Anna what had happened. Their feet kicked up dust, and the gusty wind lifted it and then let go and dumped it on their heads.

Anna said, "Well, if anyone can get us there it will be Miss Shedd. But sometimes it looks pretty well impossible. Look."

Samira looked ahead. The road had been climbing uphill steadily for the past day or two and now in the distance she could see nothing but mountains.

"Where does the road go? I can't see it at all," she said.

"See that faint brown line? We'll be up there before long, if we make it."

"Of course we'll make it," said Samira crossly. "We can't turn back now. Look how far we've come."

She flung her arm out and turned to point back along the road, then stopped as if her arm had turned to stone.

"What is it?" said Anna.

"It's men on horses. Many horses. Coming fast!"

She shaded her eyes to see better, but the horses were raising so much dust that the riders could not be seen clearly. Up and down the line boys and girls were stopping and turning. Now they could hear voices rising out of the whirl of dust.

Some of the children dropped to the ground and covered their heads. Samira could hear a thin, screeching voice cry out, "It's the Kurds! Tell them the war's over. It's the Kurds."

But as she listened to the shouts from inside the cloud of dust, Samira knew that it wasn't Kurds. It wasn't soldiers.

Suddenly she cried out, "It's the boys! It's our boys. They have found us."

Within moments the horsemen were so close that everyone could see that it was their own boys. Children were calling out, "There's Maruse. There's Matthew."

Then Samira saw Benyamin. He was standing up in the stirrups looking over the crowd of children. She waved madly and he saw her. He got off the horse so quickly that he nearly stumbled, but he caught himself and ran over to Samira.

"You're all right!" he said and gave her a hug.

"So are you," said Samira. She looked at him. "Did you think something might happen to us?"

"Of course," he said. "We weren't here to help. But you're all fine!"

"Are you disappointed?" asked Anna, but she smiled. Samira knew that she was glad to see Benyamin, too.

"Where's Ashur?" Samira asked.

"I'm right here," said Ashur. "We all made it. Now I'm checking to see that no one in the Rooftop Family got lost along the way. Everyone's here but Malik, I see. I guess he hasn't changed."

Samira started to answer but she saw Miss Shedd coming. She was walking among the children, greeting each boy. When she got to Benyamin and Ashur she reached out to clasp their hands.

"Welcome to our caravan," she said. "You did well to

catch up, even on horseback. Now the chavadar will take the horses back to Hamadan and you'll have to walk with the rest of us."

"How much longer is the journey?" asked Ashur.

"We've come almost half way. The next part will be harder because we're coming into the mountains and the road will be steep. You got here just in time." She smiled at the boys again and moved on.

"Just in time, indeed," said Anna. "Why did it take you so long?"

"The permit didn't come for a whole week," said Benyamin. "We nearly went crazy thinking you would need us and we might never get away from Hamadan. When we finally could go we were a whole week behind you. Even on horseback we were afraid we wouldn't catch up until Tabriz."

Miss Shedd came back riding on Sumbul.

"We have to keep going, children," she said. "We have a village baking bread for us and a good camping place. Save your stories for evening."

As the line started to move, Samira could feel a change in mood. Every family had been feeling the gap left by their older boys. Now they were together, and even though the road grew steeper and steeper, their feet were lighter.

She looked around at her own family. Elias was hanging on Benyamin's arm and Avram was keeping pace with Ashur.

Malik was not with the others. He had stayed faithfully with the family all the way from Hamadan. Until now.

"Do you see Malik?" she asked Anna.

Anna shook her head. "Maybe he thinks we don't need

him now that the big boys are here. He'll come back when it's time to eat. He knows he belongs with us."

Samira wasn't so sure. Malik had cheese and dried fruit in his bag just like everyone else. He wouldn't need food until they stopped for the night. Where would he be then? She worried all day.

"Why are you so quiet?" Benyamin asked her. "I was looking forward to all your questions."

"It's Malik," said Samira. "He's gone off on his own just the way he used to. This whole journey he's been different. He's been with us, helping all the time."

"How has he been helping?" asked Benyamin.

"He deals with the chavadar and helps load the mules. The mules listen to him and never make trouble when he's there, so even our mean chavadar likes him. And Malik keeps track of all the children in our family. If one strays off the road or sits down for a rest Malik is always right there. He's never let anyone get lost or left behind."

"Like a shepherd," said Benyamin.

"Yes," said Samira. "It's because he really was a shepherd before he had to leave his home. I think he spent most of his time away from his village, with the sheep. He has no father, he says, but I don't know what that means."

Benyamin frowned. "It probably means that his father went away and left him and his mother."

"He never says anything about his mother. He lived with his grandmother," said Samira.

"So he had no parents and the village didn't like him," said Benyamin. "Like the boy with the donkey in Ayna. Remember him?"

"Yes," said Samira. "I never really paid attention to him. He was just there."

"We didn't think about him. We didn't talk to him. He was nobody to us and we don't even know why."

"Well, Malik is someone to us now," said Samira. "He has to come back."

The road climbed, up and up. They made a rest stop in the afternoon and Samira turned around and saw the great dry plains spread out below her.

"We've walked all that way," she said in amazement.

"I came the easy way, on horseback," said Benyamin. "Even that was quite a journey."

It was nearly dark when they stopped, but the cook wagon was ready with hot stew and everyone hurried to get ready for dinner. By the time the Rooftop children had washed up, someone had laid out the mats and quilts.

"Did you get the bedding?" Samira asked Benyamin.

"No," he said. "When I found the chavadar the mules were already unloaded. I came back here and everything was done."

"It was Malik," said Elias. "I saw him."

"That's good," said Benyamin. "We're going to need him. Miss Shedd told me that Ashur and I will have to help with the heavy wagons from here on. We'll be going up and down real mountains now, and they could get stuck or go off the road. We won't have much time to be here for the family."

But the next morning Malik was nowhere to be seen.

Benyamin and Ashur were beginning to roll up the sleeping mats and quilts when Miss Shedd came by.

"This will be a hard day. It will be mostly downhill. That

might sound easy but the road is narrow and you'll have to walk carefully. You don't want to stumble and fall into a ravine. Ashur and Benyamin, you'll help with the wagons so they don't roll downhill too fast. The rest of you must look after each other. I know I can count on the Rooftop Family. You girls and Malik and Avram have managed everything so well."

She looked over the heads of the children grouped around her as she spoke. Samira turned and followed the direction of her gaze. There was Malik standing a little distance away. She waved at him but his whole attention was on Miss Shedd. She smiled briefly at all the children, including Malik, and then walked briskly away.

Malik went straight to the Rooftop Family's sleeping space and picked up a big pile of rolled bedding.

He grinned at Benyamin and said, "Come on. I'll show you where our mules are."

Samira breathed a deep sigh and said to Anna, "Malik is back."

"Thank goodness," said Anna. "We need him to help keep these silly children from falling into a crevasse."

Anna was right. The road went along the side of a deep, narrow valley. In some places the children had to walk in single file. Samira's legs ached from bracing herself on the steep downward slope, and progress was slow.

By the time they reached their camping place in an old caravanserai beside a river, it was nearly dark. Everyone sat around complaining about aching muscles, especially Benyamin and Ashur. They had been walking behind the cook wagon holding onto chains to slow the heavy wagon down.

"I ache in completely different places than I did after

seven days on horseback," said Benyamin, rubbing one of his shoulders and then the other. "But I do have good news. Miss Shedd says that we will stay here tomorrow. We can wash ourselves in the river and wash some clothes, too. And rest a bit before we start up the next mountain."

Everyone knew what a bathing and washing stop meant. The girls would bathe in the river first, wearing their long cotton shirts. The big girls would help the little girls, of course, handing out the soap and seeing that everyone got clean from hair to toenails. There would be time for splashing around, too. Afterward the cotton shirts would be thrown in the big kettles of hot water to be washed with the other clothes, and the girls would put on their least dirty clothes for the rest of the day.

When the girls were finished they would go and play while the boys bathed.

Luckily the next day was quite warm. The younger girls shrieked at the coolness of the water and splashed and giggled when the older ones tried to get them to stand still to be washed.

Anna finally said, "Well, I guess we'll say you are all clean."

They were standing on the riverbank, dripping, when Miss Shedd came along.

"You little girls go up to the camp and play. The women will watch over you. You bigger ones can go for a swim in peace now. The boys have gone farther down the river."

Samira walked back into the water. It moved gently around her, and she wondered what the river would look like in the dry season.

That's when she remembered that she had been in this place before. This was the river near Sain Kala.

She looked up the river. She could see water flowing down from the mountain into the pool where she was standing. When she had been here in the hot summer it had been no more than a trickle of water meandering between rocky, muddy riverbanks full of caves and holes.

We must leave your mother here above the river.

She remembered how they had lifted the bundle that was her mother and laid her in the hole they had dug.

She remembered that they said a prayer, but she couldn't remember the words.

It hadn't happened right here, she thought, but farther up, where the channel was narrower.

Samira came out of the water and, with her long shirt dripping around her, began to make her way up the river. There was a path along the stream, and soon she was out of sight of the children and the mules and the cooking fires and the caravanserai.

She came around a bend and there was Miss Shedd, sitting on a rock on the muddy bank of the river.

For a moment she seemed not to notice Samira, but then she said, "Why did you come up here? You should be playing with the others."

"I've come to see the place where my mother is buried. It was somewhere by this river but it all looks different now." She began to cry.

Miss Shedd said gently, "Sit down, Samira. There's room here on this rock."

They were both silent for a moment. Samira stopped

Celia Barker Lottridge

crying and listened to the sound of the river flowing.

"Did your mother die here?" Miss Shedd asked.

"She died on the road but they buried her near the river. We put stones on her grave. I can't see them now."

"But you were with her when she died?"

"Yes."

Miss Shedd reached out and took Samira's hand. She had never done anything like that before.

"My father is buried here, too," she said. "He was like your mother. He got sick and died during that flight."

Samira could hardly understand what Miss Shedd was saying.

"Your father was with us when we ran away?"

"Yes. He came from the mission in Urmieh. During the war he tried to help the Assyrian people as much as he could. When the area became too dangerous for the Assyrians he came away with them. He hoped to see that people got to safety. But he died near Sain Kala."

Samira sat quiet for a long time. Then she said, "You were in America."

"Yes. I got letters from my father so I knew how bad things were here. I wanted to help but the war kept me away. Then I heard that my father had died. I couldn't see him again. But I remembered the people I had grown up with and I remembered the city and the villages. So I always looked for a way to come back. When I saw a notice saying they needed a director for the orphanage for Assyrian children at Hamadan, I knew that was me. I was lucky. I came back."

Samira sat looking at the river. "If you were in America

when your father died, how do you know he is buried right here?"

"My stepmother told me. She was with him. My own mother died much earlier. But my stepmother was here and she did not die. She came back later to look for my father's bones, to take them to Urmieh to bury them properly. But nothing could be found."

Samira shivered. Her wet shirt was cold on her back.

Miss Shedd let go of her hand.

"Go and put on dry clothes and get warm by the fire. It's good that we can see where your mother and my father were laid to rest. It doesn't matter exactly where they are now. We will remember them, won't we?"

"Yes," said Samira. "I remember the picture of your father that was on your desk at the orphanage. He had nice eyes. I don't have a picture of my mother but her eyes were beautiful and she always wore a blue scarf. That's what I remember."

When Samira returned to the camp it was loud with the voices of children. She could smell the smoke of the fire and the stew cooking. The sleeping mats were neatly laid out inside the shelters, and the washed clothes were hanging on lines nearby.

"Mama," she thought, "I'm going back to Ayna. I have food and a place to sleep and people who will help me if I need it. Just the way you would help me. I think you would be glad."

Before dark Samira took Benyamin to the place where Mama was buried.

"They put her above the river and covered her," she told

Celia Barker Lottridge

him. "I don't know the exact place. I know I stood on this bank of this river and watched."

"Mama would be glad that we are here together now," said Benyamin.

"I think she would be surprised that we're going home. Back then it seemed like the end of everything."

"I know. I felt that way when I was alone in the mountains. Papa was gone and I didn't know whether I would ever see you and Mama again. Or even whether I could find my way. But this time I know that we can make the journey. It's not the end."

AFTER SAIN KALA there were some golden days when the sun shone and the road leading them along the mountains was not steep, uphill or downhill. They had been on the road for three weeks now. Samira began to feel that she could spend the rest of her life moving along with the Rooftop Family, talking and singing and looking forward to camping for the night.

One day she walked beside Malik. He no longer ran along the road guiding stray children, but she saw that he still watched constantly to be sure everyone was keeping up.

"You don't seem to be working so hard these days," she said.

"I don't have to. The young ones remember to stay on the road now, and they're used to walking all day so they don't stop unless we all stop. But sometimes they get tired and I have to help them keep up with everyone else."

Samira didn't want the conversation to end so she said, "Did you help people on the road when you left your village?"

"I was alone at the beginning. Later I caught up with other people but I didn't know them."

"Why were you alone? Didn't other people leave at the same time?"

Malik was quiet for so long that Samira thought he wouldn't answer.

Then he said, "It was my grandmother. The other people in the village were leaving and I tried to get her to come, too. She said that she would rather die at home than in some strange place. I said that if she stayed I would stay, too. But she packed up some food and a knife and an extra shirt. She handed me the bundle and said, 'Go, Malik. Life will be better for you somewhere else.' Then she went into the house and locked the door. Everyone else in the village had gone so I traveled alone. I don't know what happened to my grandmother."

He walked silently for a minute, then suddenly pointed ahead and said, "Elias and David are trying to trip each other up. I'd better stop them."

He dashed off. Samira wasn't surprised. She had never heard Malik say so much. She watched him run up to the little boys and lift Elias and then David into the air, making them laugh. Then he said a few words to them and they all walked on down the road together.

Later she told Anna about Malik's story.

"He's always had to do things on his own. No wonder he used to try to get away from this crowd." She pointed at the long line of children ahead of them.

"What will happen to him next?" said Anna. "By now he probably has no one to go home to. But then, what will happen to any of us?"

That night clouds blew in and the next day started badly, with a heavy mist that took all the warmth out of the air and left the children's clothes soggy and heavy. Gradually the mist turned to cold rain.

The road got steeper and the rain fell harder. Samira began to feel that she could hardly move her feet.

"How can I be so tired before lunch," she thought crossly. Then she looked down and saw that her shoes were thickly coated with mud. She was lifting a mud brick with every step.

Miss Shedd came by on Sumbul and looked down at the Rooftop Family.

"I'm sorry this is so hard," she said. "Even Sumbul is having trouble." She pointed to his hoofs lifting a big ball of mud with every step. "We'll get through today and then it won't be long before we start going down into the valley that leads to Tabriz. Just keep your chins up and keep going."

Samira found it impossible not to look down at her feet squishing into the mud, but she did keep going. The younger children didn't seem to mind the mud so much but they were getting cold, and it was impossible to go faster to warm up a little.

Miss Shedd came by again.

"Stop for a few minutes and eat your lunch. That will —"

She stopped and listened intently. Then they all heard the sound of hoofs coming along the trail toward them. They had passed a few strings of mules as they traveled, but these were horses, galloping fast.

Everyone stopped walking. Samira could feel her body wanting to run or crouch down to hide, but the sound was louder now and there were voices, too. There was no time to do anything but jump to the side to get out of the way.

Suddenly a horse and rider appeared. The horse was black. Samira was sure of that. But the rider seemed to be clothed in white mist. In his hand he held the pole of a green banner.

He did not look down at the children or at Miss Shedd sitting on Sumbul. He looked over his shoulder and called to someone behind him. Then he was gone, and another horse followed and another, each bearing a misty rider carrying a banner of green silk.

There were ten or twelve of them. Samira lost count.

When they were all gone, Samira felt her heart pounding in her chest. Looking down, she saw that her hands were trembling, and she reached out and found Elias and pulled him close. She wondered whether the sound of horses' hoofs would always bring to her mind the picture of soldiers galloping along a line of people, firing their guns.

Miss Shedd was looking down the road after the riders. They had disappeared around a curve.

"Were they ghosts?" Elias asked. "They were all white but their horses were real. I could smell them."

"They weren't ghosts," said Miss Shedd. "They're pilgrims going to a Muslim shrine. That's why they were carrying green banners. They weren't interested in us at all. But we do have something to worry about. They were white, all right. White with snow! We're heading into a snowstorm and we had better get going. We need to get to shelter for the night."

As they got underway the rain started again, but before long it wasn't rain anymore. It was snow. It clung to the children's clothes just as it had clung to the cloaks of the pilgrims. Pretty soon they all looked like ghosts.

Benyamin came to find Samira.

"I didn't think things could get any worse," he said, "but we've caught up with the cook wagon and it's stuck in the mud. Miss Shedd says we have to bring the pots of stew with us and keep going. We'll come back and push the wagon out in the morning."

When they finally got to the camping place, they found only one building with a roof. All the others were nothing but sagging walls. The outriders had built a small fire in a corner where it could burn in spite of the snow. The cook put the big stew pots in the ashes to warm, and the big boys and girls started setting up the tents.

Snow got into folds in the canvas and down the backs of the children's necks, but at last the tents were up and there was hot water for tea. Samira thought she had never tasted anything so good. When the stew was finally dished out it was barely warm, but just having it in her belly was comforting.

When the stew was gone and the cups were washed, everyone was ready to sleep. Only the sleeping mats and quilts had been unpacked, so the children took off their jackets and shoes and crawled under the quilts with their other clothes on.

The girls moved as close together as they could to share their warmth. Samira thought she would never stop being cold, but when she woke in the morning she found herself sandwiched between Shula and Monna and so cozy that she hated to get up.

Before she could quite get up the courage to pull herself

out from under the covers, Miss Shedd came to the opening of the tent.

"You needn't jump out of bed. It's not snowing anymore but it's going to take a few hours to get the cook wagon out of the ditch, so we'll not be going on today. There will be tea and breakfast in an hour or so. The snow will melt. It's not winter yet."

The children tried to go back to sleep, but they were so used to getting up before dawn that they just couldn't do it. They kept sitting up and then lying down again until Anna said, "We're like a pot trying to bubble. Best to get it over with. Everyone up!"

Once they were all out of bed Samira looked around at the girls of the Rooftop Family and thought, "We are a pretty sorry-looking bunch. Our clothes are wrinkled and we're muddy and our hair is sticking up every which way. What will they think of us in Tabriz?"

She and Anna got everyone brushed off, and then Anna went off for a pot of warm water so that all faces could be washed.

Everything seemed to take a very long time that day. The sky was gray and a mist rising from the snowy mountainside made it impossible to see down the road in either direction. After breakfast Benyamin and Ashur and some of the other boys went off to get the cook wagon out of the mud. They took four mules with them.

Benyamin said to Malik, "We need you to come and talk to the mules so they'll pull their best for us."

"They will," said Malik, and he actually grinned before he disappeared into the whiteness with the other boys.

"At least they have something to do," said Anna. "What can we do? I'm out of stories and no one wants to play any of the games."

"I know," said Samira. "Let's braid all the girls' hair. No one has done it for days."

"And those people in Tabriz might think a little better of us if we're properly braided," said Anna.

They settled themselves where they could see the road, and one by one girls from all the families came and sat in front of Samira or Anna. They carefully loosened the tangled braids and combed out the snarls. When each girl was finished she was content to sit and watch another head of hair being neatly braided.

It was afternoon before the boys triumphantly arrived with the cook wagon. The cook was sitting in his usual place, holding the reins and smiling broadly.

"It was quite a job to get us out of the mud," he told everyone around the fire. "It took every boy pushing and Malik making every mule pull. Then we had to take one of the wheels off and pound it back into shape. It was so bent it wouldn't turn. But we lost nothing. We're getting low on food, though. Lentils and onions for tonight and for tomorrow, beans. Then we had better get to Tabriz."

It really wasn't quite so desperate. The outriders brought bread and enough eggs that each child could have half a hard-boiled egg for lunch the next day. Still, Samira knew she was ready for something different. Pickled cucumbers, maybe. Or rice pilaf with chicken. Or really, really hot soup.

She rubbed her cold hands and thought about hot soup.

"It won't be long," she promised herself.

The next day the sun shone, but frost glittered on the grass and there was a thin skin of ice on the bucket of water Samira had filled the night before. When Miss Shedd made her rounds she said that the cold was a good thing.

"The mud won't be so sticky," she said. "We should make better time. Unless something else goes wrong we'll camp just one more night before we get to Tabriz."

With that promise everyone walked briskly. The road went downhill, sometimes gently and sometimes quite steeply.

The feeling of reaching the end of the journey made everyone a little giddy, and they laughed and sang as they walked. Malik found two sticks and beat them together to the rhythm of the songs.

"Remember, we have to keep walking all day," he reminded Elias and David, who were racing to see who could reach the next bend first.

When the travelers reached the caravanserai, they saw that it was a good one with enough roofs for everyone to sleep under shelter. Their high spirits even affected the chavadars, who unloaded the bedding and laid it out before the children got to the mule enclosure. The boys found dry willow branches along a stream and made a larger fire than usual, and the cook, in spite of his prediction of plain bean soup, produced a delicious lamb stew.

"Some angel delivered meat to me," he said, and Miss Shedd smiled.

When the stew was gone she passed around a big tin filled with sugared almonds.

"I've been saving them for our last night. It's been a long journey and we all deserve a treat."

Samira ate her share slowly. They made her think of the almonds stored in the umbar in Ayna. And the tree where the almonds grew.

When all the almonds were gone Miss Shedd said, "I want to tell you what will happen when we get to Tabriz. In the city there's a boys' orphanage and a girls' orphanage so you will not all be in one place. I'm sorry that the families can't stay together but the two orphanages are right next to each other and I'll make sure you get to see each other often. Remember that you will only be in Tabriz over the winter. I'll start working on getting you home as soon as you're all settled and going to school."

She stopped speaking and everyone was quiet. They had gotten so used to being together on the road that it was hard to think about being inside buildings and separated.

On the last day of the journey the wagons, the line of children and the mules all started out at dawn. The family groups stayed together but now and then a child would dart along the edge of the road, looking for a special friend in another family.

When Miss Shedd came by she said, "You'll have plenty of time together. You don't have to say goodbye."

Anna came to walk beside Samira. "If they find a home for either of us we'll have to say goodbye," she said. "When that happens we'll probably never see each other again."

Samira looked down the line of children walking toward Tabriz. If each one could suddenly go home they would end up walking in a hundred different directions, not together at all.

"If we could have stayed in the orphanage in Hamadan

none of us would have to be separated. Would that be better?"

"Maybe," said Anna. "It was a kind of home, and none of us knows what home we will find when Miss Shedd sends us on from Tabriz. She says that we all have family. Maybe some of us don't."

"I hope I'll have some family," said Samira. "My aunt or my cousins. But it won't be the family I had before."

"You know more than I do," said Anna sadly. "I was away from my village when we had to leave. I never found out what happened to my mother and my sisters. Maybe they went to a different camp. I'm afraid to hope but I do hope."

Anna had never spoken about what had happened to her family. Now Samira knew that Anna's story was different from hers. She might even find her mother or her sisters.

Samira could not hope for that. Her mother would not be waiting for her and neither would her father or Maryam. Her hope was to find Aunt Sahra or someone in Ayna who would remember her and Benyamin.

In spite of all the questions Samira could feel her spirits lifting. She knew that not very far away was the big lake, Lake Urmieh, that she had heard about all her life. Now she could imagine that she would see it and even cross it in a boat and return to Ayna.

At midday a group of men and women from the orphanages and schools in Tabriz came on horseback to meet the travelers. Miss Shedd was riding at the head of the caravan on Sumbul. She wore a dark blue jacket and a scarf striped with many shades of red wrapped around her head and shoulders. The children had never seen these fine clothes before.

Samira suddenly remembered the men of Ayna putting on their finest coats and riding to meet expected guests, to greet them and honor them.

"She must have brought that jacket especially for this day," she said to Anna. "I'm glad we braided the girls' hair. We don't look fine but we aren't a disgrace, either."

"Will they talk for a long time?" asked Elias. He was watching Miss Shedd and the people from Tabriz exchanging greetings. Samira thought he was right to be worried. When grownups were being polite they could talk for a very long time.

This time, however, they did not, and all the children were pleased to see that the welcomers had brought big baskets with them. They spread out trays of grape leaves rolled up around meat and rice, bread spread with jam, sticky dates and little cakes made with almonds.

"This is not what we eat every day," warned the director of the girls' orphanage with a smile. "It's a special picnic to welcome you to Tabriz."

After lunch Miss Shedd spoke to the whole group.

"The people of Tabriz and everyone in the orphanages want to welcome us to the city. We aren't far now so brush yourselves off and look as tidy as you can. Boys, you walk on the left side of the road and girls on the right. That way you won't have to sort yourselves out when we reach the two buildings."

Benyamin was sitting near Samira. When he heard the word orphanage he stirred restlessly and said to her in a low voice, "I'm seventeen. I don't think I belong in an orphanage."

Samira was surprised. Where else could he go?

But there was no time to talk. It was time to move on to Tabriz.

When they got to the city the sides of the streets were so crowded with welcoming people that Samira saw nothing but smiling faces until they came to an open square with two big buildings on one side. Lined up in front of the buildings were many children neatly dressed in uniforms.

When they saw the travelers they began to sing, and Miss Shedd led the caravan children forward to the buildings. Then the girls went up the steps of the building on the right and the boys went up the steps of the building on the left.

Samira looked around at Anna and Maryam and Monna and all the girls of the Rooftop Family and the other families. After thirty days of walking together under the sky they were going through tall wooden doors into a new part of their lives.

Before she crossed the threshold she turned toward the boys' building. No one was left on the steps. Like magic Benyamin, Elias, David, Malik, Avram and Ashur were gone.

FIVE

*Wait for
the Morning Star*

Tabriz Orphanage
November 1923

THE GIRLS stood crowded into the dim front hall of the orphanage. A woman standing halfway up a staircase talked to them about baths and clean clothes.

Anna whispered in Samira's ear, "Just like going into the camp at Baqubah."

But it really wasn't. For one thing the water was wonderfully hot. For another their clothes weren't taken away and burned.

"Your clothes are a little worn but they are perfectly good," said a woman as she handed out new clothes. "You can mend them and keep them to wear when you go home. For now you'll wear the uniform of the orphanage."

The uniform was a white blouse, a dark blue skirt and jacket and a blue headscarf. The clothes made Samira remember Mrs. McDowell and the green dresses, all alike. She wished that Mrs. McDowell could know that she and Anna were in Tabriz, almost ready for the last step that would take them home.

Hot water was not the only luxury. The soup they had for supper was really hot, too, and there was a bowl of sliced cucumbers and onions on every table. The first fresh vegetables the children had had in a month.

The Hamadan girls were pleased with the new clothes

and hot soup, but when they saw the dormitories where they would sleep, they were uneasy. There were no familiar sleeping mats to unroll. Instead the long rooms had beds lined up along each wall, and each bed had another bed above it.

There was no word for such beds in Syriac, so the matron told them the English word. Bunk beds.

"I can't sleep up in the air," Samira whispered to Anna. "I'll fall off and break my bones."

She was not the only one to feel that way. When it was time to go to bed the caravan girls, without any talking, arranged to sleep so that each bunk bed had one big girl and one small girl, and the two girls both slept in the bottom bed.

One evening Samira looked down the line of bunk beds and thought, "I used to sleep on a roof. Surely I can sleep on the top bed."

She settled Monna in the bottom bed, saying, "I'll be right above you if you need me." Then she climbed up and slept soundly all night.

The other girls waited a few nights to make sure Samira wasn't going to fall off. Then they stopped crowding each other in the lower bed and took turns sleeping up and down.

"We shouldn't get too used to these fancy beds," said Anna. "If we do get back to our villages we'll be sleeping on the ground again."

"That will be easy," said Samira.

It was not easy to get used to the organized life of Tabriz Orphanage. There was less work than in Hamadan but more schooling. Each day the children had lessons in the morning and training in the afternoon. Training meant learning to do something that could earn some money in the future. Samira was learning to be a teacher of children just beginning school, or at least a teacher's assistant, and Anna was learning to be a nurse's aide.

After training came outdoor games and circle dancing. Sometimes the boys and girls played together, but they were expected to keep the games going so there was not much time for visiting. Being told what to do most of the time made Samira restless.

"I miss having time to talk and be with our friends," she said to Anna one day. "And you know what? I miss our caravan."

"I know what you mean. Watch Elias and Malik when you see them on Sunday. You can see how much they miss being outdoors."

It was on Sundays after church that the caravan families could gather in the big square or in the boys' dining hall if the weather was bad. Nothing organized, just a chance to be with friends.

The next Sunday Samira watched Malik and Elias chase each other through the groups of children. Malik was faster, of course, but Elias was small and quick. He could sometimes dodge around a corner and come back and surprise Malik.

The rest of the Rooftop Family was happy to sit and talk together.

Miss Shedd usually spent some time with the caravan children during these gatherings, but she was now director of both the boys' and the girls' orphanages so she was even busier than she had been in Hamadan. Often she had to rush off to a meeting, but she always made sure that each caravan family had a chance to be together before she left.

Then one Sunday Miss Shedd did not hurry off. She sat with the children in the boys' dining hall and spoke to all of them.

"I miss the days when we were getting our caravan organized and when we were out on the road together," she said. "We all got to Tabriz but our purpose was to get you home and you aren't home yet. Miss Sabat, one of the teachers, is ready to go across the lake as soon as the weather warms up. She will visit the villages to try to find your family members or friends. Your job is to be patient. You have the rest of the winter to work hard at your school lessons and training so when it's time for you to go home you'll be ready to be useful, and the people in the villages will be glad to welcome you."

After Miss Shedd left, Samira saw Benyamin coming toward her. He looked tall and serious.

"You look as if you have bad news," she said.

Benyamin looked past her out the window.

"It's not bad news but I know you're not going to like it..." His voice trailed off.

"Just tell me," Samira said. She had a cold feeling that she knew what he was going to say.

Benyamin looked straight at her now. "Ashur and I have decided not to go back to our villages. We want to leave the orphanage but we'll stay here in Tabriz in a lodging with some of the others our age and go on with our schooling. We want to do more in the world than tend vines or take care of sheep. Miss Shedd says it's a good plan but I need to know that you understand. Do you?"

Samira's head could understand, but the words that spilled out of her came from somewhere else.

"Not go home! How can you even think of not going home? We're a family and we're supposed to stay together. Don't you remember?"

Benyamin sat down on a bench and pulled her down beside him. He was quiet for a long time.

Then he said, "Yes, I remember. I was fifteen when I said that, and I couldn't imagine living anywhere but Ayna. Now I'm almost eighteen. I see that there are other places to live, other lives to live. I can't go back. Not to stay."

Samira looked down at Benyamin's hand pressing hard into the wooden bench. His fingers were long and strong. He was not a boy anymore.

"But what will I do? I thought we would go to Ayna together. I don't think I could stay in Tabriz. My life couldn't be here."

"No," said Benyamin. "You really want to go to Ayna. Miss Shedd will find out who is there for you. If there's no one we'll make another plan. I won't leave you alone. I'm your brother."

Samira could see that Benyamin had decided. She could only wait to see what would happen to her.

The winter passed slowly. When the wind felt almost warm and the bushes around the courtyard began to show little green leaves, Miss Sabat set off on her first journey to find homes for the caravan orphans. She was going up into the mountains on this trip so Samira and Anna knew there would be no news for them.

When Miss Sabat returned, Shula, Avram, Maryam and

Malik, who came from mountain villages, were called to a meeting. They would hear news of what she had found.

Samira, Anna, Benyamin and Ashur were waiting in the hall when children began to crowd out of the room. Maryam hurried over to them.

"She brought a letter from my father's cousin welcoming me home. I didn't believe it could happen but it did."

Avram and Shula had good news, too, and they all rushed off full of excitement.

But Malik did not come out.

"Let's go in," said Benyamin. He pushed the door open and the others followed him into the room. They saw Malik standing in front of Miss Sabat shaking his head.

"My grandmother? How do you know it was my grandmother? It must be a mistake."

Miss Sabat tried to answer him but Malik kept shaking his head and saying, "How do you know?" louder and louder until he was shouting.

Miss Sabat stepped away from Malik and motioned the other children to come near. Malik stopped shouting and just stood looking dazed.

"You're friends of Malik, aren't you?" Miss Sabat asked. They all nodded.

"I found Malik's grandmother. She managed to stay alive in her village these five years. She wants Malik to come home but he can't believe I really saw her. I think he made up his mind that she had died."

Malik suddenly stepped between Samira and Benyamin and said to Miss Sabat, "Did she give you something to show that she's really my grandmother?"

"No," said Miss Sabat. "But she gave me some words to say to you. Do you want to hear them?"

"Yes," said Malik.

"She said, 'Tell my grandson to wait for the morning star to rise before he sets out on his journey.'"

Malik looked up and met Miss Sabat's eyes. He took a deep breath and squared his shoulders.

"You have seen my grandmother. That is what she always said when I was going out very early in the morning to take the sheep into the hills. I thought she would be dead by now but I was wrong. I will go home."

He turned and looked at his friends.

"Goodbye," he said. Then he reached out and clasped each one of them by the hand.

"Goodbye," he said again. Then he was out the door.

"Why did he say goodbye?" asked Anna. "Surely he won't be going right away."

"He will," said Miss Sabat. "I'm leaving tomorrow to visit more villages and a few of the children have permits to cross the lake with me. He's one of them and it seems that he's ready to go."

"He's made up his mind," said Samira, almost to herself. "He'll go tomorrow."

But she could hardly believe she would not see Malik coming around the corner unexpectedly one day with his long legs and uncombed hair. She felt a hole inside her somewhere. And this was just the beginning.

THE CELEBRATIONS that came with the Persian spring were just over when Samira and Anna stood in the parlor of the girls' orphanage waiting for Miss Sabat. She had just returned from traveling to villages in the hills around the city of Urmieh, and she had sent a message asking the two girls to meet with her.

. They were too nervous to sit down. Whatever Miss Sabat had to tell them was serious. It could not wait for a meeting of all the children from the area she had visited. Samira found herself braiding and unbraiding the fringe at the end of her scarf, and Anna was twisting her fingers into one knot after another.

It seemed a long time before the young teacher came through the door. She asked them to sit down on a bench, speaking in a gentle voice that made Samira feel worried.

She looked from one girl to the other.

"I wanted to talk to you girls together because I have been told that you are very good friends." Then she looked only at Anna. "Most of the villages I went to this time are somewhat ruined, but people are there and they are rebuilding their lives. But I'm sad to tell you, Anna, that your village was really destroyed. No one could tell me what happened to any of the people from your village. And no one has returned." She put out both her hands as if she wanted to comfort Anna and then clasped them in front of her.

Anna was looking past her, out the parlor door and down the long hall.

"I kept thinking my mother or maybe one of my sisters might be alive," she said. "I wasn't there when the soldiers came. I was in another village helping my aunt with her new baby. I couldn't go home so I ran away with them."

"And your aunt?' asked Miss Sabat.

"No," said Anna. And she began to cry, big sobs bursting from her.

Samira had never seen Anna cry, and she didn't know what to do. But Miss Sabat took Anna by the hand and led her to a comfortable chair and said, "You cry. We are here with you."

After a bit Anna's sobs changed to gasping breaths. When she could speak she said, "All these years in the camps and the orphanages I've had a tiny thought that someone might be alive. I was so foolish."

"No," said Miss Sabat. "Hope is never foolish. It helped you remember the people you love and that is good." She stopped for a moment and then said, "I could tell you Samira's news. Would you both like to hear it?"

Anna said, "Yes. It must be better than mine."

Miss Sabat looked at Samira. "I found your Aunt Sahra. She is in Ayna with Ester, your cousin. Your other cousin died in the city during the massacres. I'm very sorry about that. But your aunt and your cousin are overjoyed that you are well and they're waiting for you to come home."

Samira was quiet for a moment while the good news settled in her mind. Aunt Sahra and Ester. Ester would be twelve years old now. Did they live in their old house? Were the almond trees blooming now, in spring?

She suddenly realized that Miss Sabat was talking to Anna.

"You'll need time to think about what you want to do, but Miss Shedd and I have an idea. You've been training to be a nurse's aide. You could go to the city of Urmieh and work at the hospital there. There's a residence for the nurses and

Celia Barker Lottridge

nurses' aides so you could live safely among people who would be your friends."

Anna sat hunched in the chair and was silent. Samira went and stood beside her.

"Think about it," Miss Sabat said after a moment. "I must go but you girls can stay here in the parlor as long as you want."

As soon as she was gone, Anna said in a low, fierce voice, "I won't live in a city in a residence. It would be like an orphanage again. They can't make me."

"You wouldn't be so far from Ayna," said Samira. "Maybe I could come and visit you."

"Once you get to your village you won't have time to go away for visits. You know that."

"Yes," said Samira. Anna was right. She knew how much work there would be.

"I'm going home," she thought. "But without Mama and Papa? Without Maryam and Benyamin? How can it be home?"

She did have Aunt Sahra and Ester. Anna had no one. That could not be right. She had been Samira's family ever since they had put their sleeping mats side by side in the tent in Baqubah.

Suddenly Samira was standing in front of Anna.

"Do you still have that piece of paper? The letter signed by a British officer?"

Anna stared at her. "Of course I do. It's in my caravan bag. Why?"

"I want you to come with me to Ayna. That letter says we must never be separated. Do you want to come to Ayna with me?"

Anna took a deep breath. "I had such hope that my mother and my sisters would still be alive. In my head they were there in our house waiting for me. But it was only in my head. Not real. You are real. I'll go to Ayna."

Samira felt a wave of relief go through her.

"Let's get the letter."

Back in the dormitory Anna pulled her caravan bag out from under the bed. She took out a piece of cardboard stitched on three sides to make a pocket.

"When we were in Kermanshah Mr. Edwards had a notebook with cardboard covers. He was going to throw it away so I asked him for the cover. I used it to make this pocket to keep the letter safe. It's right here."

"You did the right thing," said Samira. "Now we have to see Miss Shedd. We'll show her the letter and explain that you must come with me to Ayna."

Miss Shedd was in her office sitting behind a desk littered with papers. The photograph of her father was there, propped against a pile of books.

"He's still with her, watching what she's doing," thought Samira.

"Girls," said Miss Shedd. "Sit down. I have better chairs for you than we had in Hamadan." She looked at Anna. "I'm sorry that your mother and your sisters didn't live through the troubles. But I hope that you can think about the plan Miss Sabat told you about."

Anna stood up.

"When I first came to the Baqubah camp I found Samira and we decided that we would not be separated, no matter what. If my family were alive now I would go to them. But

Celia Barker Lottridge

they are dead and Samira is my family. We want to stay together. And we have this."

She slipped the letter out of the cardboard pocket. Samira could see that it was yellowed and nearly worn through where it had been folded, but when Anna carefully smoothed it, there it was, a piece of paper with English words written on it and, at the bottom, a signature.

She felt a sudden trickle of fear. No one who read English had ever seen this paper. What did it really say? She tried to remember the nurse who said she was an officer in the British army. Was she someone to trust?

Miss Shedd was reading the paper. She looked up.

"This says that you two girls and Elias must never be separated. And it seems to be signed by an officer in the medical corps. Is that correct?"

Samira was speechless. She had forgotten that Elias was part of the document.

Anna was not speechless.

"They wanted the two of us to take charge of Elias and we said we would only do it if they promised that we would stay together. So we got this paper. We knew how the British wanted everything written down."

She looked hopefully at Miss Shedd who said, "Sit down, Anna. You are not under British protection anymore, of course. But this is an official document and I think you were very smart to get it. It means that you two and Elias have been recognized as a family and that makes it reasonable for us to keep you together. I believe that Samira's aunt would likely be glad to have both of you but Elias could be a problem. A six-year-old would be a big responsibility and not very much help. And he's doing so well in the orphanage that I think he should stay here. What do you girls think?"

Samira could feel thoughts banging around in her head. Would they have to stay here because Elias should stay? How could they leave him if it made him unhappy?

Before she could say anything, Anna said, "If Elias wants to stay here, of course he should stay. Or he could come to us later. Or maybe Samira's aunt will want him. But what about me? Do we have to ask Samira's aunt before I can go?"

Miss Shedd frowned a little and gave Anna a look that said, "There's no need to shout." Then she said, "It would take weeks of sending letters back and forth to ask Samira's aunt whether she's willing to have two girls instead of one. I think we have to take a chance and send you to Ayna with Samira. But it's not easy in the villages now. If she can't keep you will you come back without fussing?"

Anna nodded but she closed her eyes as if to shut out the picture of returning to Tabriz.

Samira was sure that the Aunt Sahra she had known so long ago would welcome Anna. But if things were very bad in Ayna maybe she would have no place for another girl.

"Aunt Sahra will want Anna," she said at last. "I'll help her make it work."

"That's all you can do," said Miss Shedd. "Can I keep this document in my file? Just in case anyone questions this decision. And will you girls speak to Elias? I don't quite know what I'll do if he wants to go with you."

As the girls left Miss Shedd's office they heard the bell that signaled that it was time to go outside for organized games.

"I can't play games today," said Anna. "I'm all up and down. I thought I might have a family. Then I had no family. Now I have a family. I have to get used to it all."

"Miss Sabat said we could stay in the parlor as long as we wanted. No one will be there."

So Anna and Samira spent the rest of the afternoon curled up in the soft cushioned chairs of the parlor. They talked a little about Ayna and what they would do there, but mostly they just sat. Samira even went to sleep for a while.

She dreamed of picking almonds and eating them while they were still milky and soft. When she woke up she thought, "Now I'll see whether the almond tree is still there."

On Sunday afternoon Samira and Anna lured Elias out for a walk by slipping some dried apricots from lunch into their pockets.

"You can eat these while we walk to the gate and back," Samira said to him. "Then you can play with your friends."

"Good," said Elias. "We have a team and I'm almost the captain. Well, not quite but I'm the fastest runner so they really need me." He went on chattering about his team that seemed to play every game Samira had ever heard of.

Finally Anna said, "Listen a minute, Elias. Soon Samira and I will take a boat across Lake Urmieh and go to live in a village with Samira's aunt."

"But we live here," said Elias.

"We do now," said Samira. "But when I was your age I used to live in that village and I want to go back. Anna is coming with me."

"Is Benyamin going?"

"No," said Samira. "He's staying here."

"I'll stay here with Benyamin."

"But you'll stay in the orphanage," said Anna. "Benyamin will live in the city."

"Benyamin can visit me," said Elias. "I'll grow up and then I'll leave. Like you. But I won't go to a village."

Samira looked at him. He was a sturdy boy. He was smart. She had known him almost all his life. But he couldn't remember anything before the camps and the orphanages. Why would he want to go to a village?

She suddenly grabbed him and gave him such a tight hug that he began to struggle to get away.

"That's so you'll remember me when I'm in the village and you're here. I'll send you some almonds. Will you write me a letter?"

Elias thought for a moment. "I will when I can write better," he said.

He gave them each a quick kiss on the cheek and ran off to find his team.

"I don't think we have to worry about Elias," said Anna. "I hope he does write. I want to know what he grows up to be."

A few weeks later all the people in the Rooftop Family who were still in Tabriz came to see Samira and Anna off on their journey. Benyamin and Ashur were there with Elias and David. Monna's grandmother had been discovered living right in Tabriz. Monna and Sheran were living with her now and she had brought the two girls to say goodbye. Shula, Avram, Maryam and Malik had already gone to their mountain villages.

But someone else was missing.

Samira looked around. Where was Miss Shedd? Surely she would come to say goodbye.

The Rooftop Family stood together in the courtyard with other children who would be returning to villages around Urmieh. Miss Sabat would soon arrive with a truck that would take them to the boat.

Seeing Benyamin standing there made Samira remember how she had seen him under the chinar trees at the end of the terrible journey. Then he had been thin and dirty. Now he was healthy and clean. And old enough to choose how he wanted to live his life.

But he was still her brother and now they had to say goodbye.

"We're each doing the right thing," he said to her. "You know that, don't you?"

Samira could only nod. If she spoke she would start to cry.

"I'll write to you and I'll come to Ayna as soon as I can and see all the good work you've done. I promise."

That was all he could say, she knew. The truck was there. She only had time to give Monna and Sheran and David a quick hug each and Elias a longer one. Then she climbed into the truck and sat down on one of the benches. Benyamin reached up and clasped her hand.

Then he lifted Elias up in his arms and everyone waved as the truck pulled out of the orphanage gates. Samira kept waving until they were out of sight.

They had not gone far when the truck suddenly stopped. In the silence Samira heard the sound of a horse coming at a brisk pace. She looked back and saw Miss Shedd riding up on Sumbul.

The children all scrambled out of the truck and Miss Shedd dismounted.

"I wanted to come and see you off when you left but I couldn't get there in time. Sumbul has been needing a good gallop so I saddled him up and here I am." She looked at Samira. "I had to come in my skirt," she said. "No time to change to my traveling clothes." And she smiled.

Samira wanted to fling her arms around Miss Shedd, but she knew that would be the wrong thing to do. Everyone would start crying and they couldn't say goodbye that way.

Miss Shedd looked around the group of children and said, "We made such a journey together. And none of it could have happened without your work and your ideas. We managed to have a good time, too. I'll remember every one of you. Now you had better get on the road. You have a long way to go today."

She put her foot in the stirrup and swung herself up onto Sumbul's back. The children crowded around.

"Goodbye, goodbye," they said and watched Miss Shedd ride away.

THE DAY did seem long, and Samira was on the verge of dozing in spite of the bumpy road when the sight of the lake roused her. It stretched away, a sheet of blue water moving up and down gently as if the lake was sleeping and quietly breathing.

They slept on the shore of the lake that night. When they woke a boat with black smoke puffing from its smokestack was waiting at the dock. In no time Samira found herself standing on its wooden deck holding tight to the rail. The boat was going up and down on the gently rolling water. It was terrible.

"I'd rather be on our caravan journey in a dust storm," she managed to say to Anna. Then she kept her mouth shut tight, determined to keep her breakfast down, and closed her eyes.

Someone came and unclenched her fingers from the railing and laid her down on a pile of canvas. When she woke up the boat was still and all the people were rushing around gathering up their things.

"You missed the whole crossing," said Anna. "I threw up once but after that I could see everything. The birds and the islands and the other boats."

Samira didn't care. She was just waiting to put her feet on solid ground.

"I guess I'll never go back to Tabriz," she said.

"Oh, yes, you will," said Miss Sabat. "You'll forget about being seasick and you'll want to see Benyamin and Elias. You're a traveler, remember."

Samira smiled but she wondered. To be a traveler you surely had to want to travel. She had never wanted to leave home at all. But she had made a great journey. She remembered the lake at Kermanshah and the view of the mountains from the Hamadan orphanage and the river at Sain Kala. There would be other things to see if she traveled farther. Maybe some day.

Right now she was busy carrying ashore the things she and Anna were taking to Ayna. Their clothes and schoolbooks, of course, but gifts for Aunt Sahra and Ester, too. A bundle of fabric, a bag of rice, a box of dried fruit, and seeds for the garden they would plant.

Miss Sabat couldn't take Samira and Anna to Ayna. She was traveling with the other children to villages that lay in another direction. Instead, Miss Grant from the Near East Relief office in the city came and camped with them beside the lake. She brought a donkey to carry the bundles and a man to take care of the donkey.

They started out early in the morning when the stars had faded away and the sun was just rising over the lake.

Samira said to Anna, "I'm glad we waited for the morning star to come and go before we started on our journey."

The road went across a flat plain and then began to climb into the hills. Miss Grant asked them many questions about their journey from Hamadan to Tabriz.

"Everyone was amazed that Miss Shedd would undertake such a journey with so little help," she said. "It was a miracle that you all made it safely."

Samira and Anna tried to explain about the caravan families and how they had all helped, but Miss Grant kept on being amazed so the girls just smiled and nodded.

Samira thought it probably was a miracle that all the children arrived safely in Tabriz. But it was a miracle that had taken a lot of hard work. She remembered Malik running up and down the line of Rooftop children, making sure they were all there.

"I wonder how Malik is," she said to Anna. "Do you think he's happy with his grandmother?"

"We'll never know," said Anna. "He certainly won't write us a letter."

"You're right," said Samira. "But I can't help wondering."

They walked for a long time in silence. Miss Grant had run out of questions but she kindly offered them dried fruit and water she carried in a bottle.

It was dusk when they got to Ayna, making Samira's first look at the village seem a little like a dream. She saw a shadowed street and she remembered it well. But it was not quite right. The houses were still standing but many of them were clearly uncared for, with clay bricks crumbling and doors hanging on their hinges.

Which was her house? There should be a roof over a terrace and a pot of flowers on a stone by the doorstep, but every house seemed to have the same blank face.

Then one of the doors opened and a woman came out. Behind her came a girl. Miss Grant stepped forward to speak to them but the woman looked past her and straight at Samira. She ran forward with her arms open.

"Oh, my dear, dear Samira. You have come home."

When she stood back Samira knew that this really was Aunt Sahra. Her face was familiar but it was thin, not round as she remembered. And she was so short.

But, no, of course, she was the one who was taller.

Ester was taller, too, not the little girl Samira remembered. She came shyly to Samira and Samira put her arms around her and Aunt Sahra hugged them both. Then she took Samira's hand as if Samira might suddenly run off, and looked at Anna.

"Aunt Sahra," said Samira. Her voice trembled. "This is my friend Anna. She has been with me this whole time. Now she has no home to go to. Her family did not survive and her village is destroyed. She has been my family all these years and we wondered…"

Aunt Sahra went to Anna, still holding Samira's hand.

"You must stay with us. I have only Ester and now Samira. I will be so glad to have you." And she let go of Samira's hand and put her arms around Anna.

It was nearly dark.

"We must unload the donkey and this man and I will need to stay here tonight," said Miss Grant.

Aunt Sahra went over to her.

"Forgive me for not greeting you and offering you the small hospitality of my house. The man will eat with us and sleep in the stable with the donkey and you, dear lady, are welcome in my poor house."

"I've brought bread and cheese from the city," said Miss Grant. "And some honey for your household. And I thank you for offering me the warmth of your house."

Suddenly Samira knew she was home. Hospitality and gifts and honoring a guest. All those things had been missing for five years. There had been kindness but not this.

She was home and Anna was home. She took Anna's hand and led her into the house.

IT WAS summer. Samira stood on the roof of the house and looked over the wall up to the hill where she and Anna had planted their garden. She didn't have to stand on tiptoe now to see the rows of tomatoes and squash and melons, and the almond tree Aunt Sahra had planted to replace the one cut down during the troubles. Soon there would good things to gather and eat, and to preserve for the winter.

She walked to the other side of the roof, noticing how smooth the clay surface was under her feet. She and Anna had spread that clay so the roof wouldn't leak anymore.

Aunt Sahra had returned to find her house damaged by water and stripped of everything that could be used for fuel. Window frames, the carved chest and even baskets were gone. Samira's house was bare, too, and part of the ceiling had fallen.

But the umbar under the terrace had not been touched.

"Most of the food was too dried out to be used," Aunt Sahra told Samira. "But your beautiful rugs are here for you."

The rugs were in Aunt Sahra's house for now, but Samira hoped that one day she could take them with her when she went to live in her family's house again.

Now she looked down into the street where she used to watch Benyamin and his friends run to school. It made her sad to think that most of those boys were gone. If they were alive, no one knew where they were. But Benyamin was fine. She had received a letter from him just the other day. His studies were going well but he and his friends found that keeping house and preparing food was hard work. Miss Shedd made sure they had the supplies they needed but they had to do all the work themselves.

When she read that part of the letter to Anna they both laughed, remembering how the boys hated kitchen duty.

In the letter there was a drawing Elias had made for her and Anna. It showed a boy with a big smile on his face waving one hand in greeting and holding a large red ball under his other arm. Aunt Sahra had pinned the drawing to the wall so the girls could look at it and smile.

Now Samira saw Anna come out the front door with Ester. They were going to clean up the old schoolroom beside the church. It was a solid stone building with a good tile roof, but inside, the floor was covered with bat droppings and broken plaster. When the place was clean and they had whitewashed the walls, Anna and Samira planned to start a school for the little children.

The priest who came to Ayna once a month was pleased with their plans.

"I'm trying to find a teacher for the older children," he said. "It's going to take some time because so many Assyrians have not come back. Or they're busy rebuilding their villages. But I won't give up."

Samira knew it was time to leave the roof and help Aunt Sahra with the bread baking, but something drew her to look at the garden again. For a moment she thought of the night she had seen the soldiers, but there were no soldiers now.

Then she did see something coming over the far hill. A fox? No, it was bigger. And it had two legs, not four. It looked like a boy or a man moving very fast. He disappeared behind the near hill. Then suddenly he was coming down past the garden.

No one ran like that except...

Malik! It was Malik.

Samira called out, "Malik, Malik, I'm here. On the roof."

Malik stopped. He looked up at her.

"Come down," he said. "Come down."

Samira had never climbed down the ladder so fast. Malik was standing at the bottom.

"I'm so glad to see you," she said. "But why are you here? You went home to your grandmother, didn't you?"

"Yes," said Malik. "She wanted to see me. To see that I was alive. She wanted me to see that she had gotten through the war. But she didn't want me to stay. She said the same thing she said when she sent me off before the soldiers came. She said, 'Malik, go. It will be better for you somewhere else.' So I came here to see whether you had come home."

"Will she be all right without you?" asked Samira.

"She's strong. She's managed all these years."

"So you came to Ayna. Will you stay? Anna is here, too, and I know my aunt will welcome you."

He was listening to her but his eyes were skipping from the house to the garden and through the gap between the houses to the village street. She knew he was thinking of the next thing he would do.

"I want to stay," he said.

"But what will you do? Could we get some sheep?"

"No more sheep," said Malik. "I'll build. I learned in trade school."

"No more sheep," agreed Samira. "But building! We need a builder and I know exactly where you can start. In my very own house. Will you come inside and look?" She was filled with joy.

"Show me," said Malik.

Where the Story Came From

My mother, Louise Shedd Barker, was born in Persia, the country now called Iran, in 1906. Her family lived near the city of Urmieh where her father, William Shedd, was an American missionary to the Assyrians, a people who have lived in northwestern Iran for thousands of years. The Assyrians speak an ancient language called Syriac or Assyrian. They have been Christians since the very early history of Christianity.

When I was growing up, my mother told me many stories about her childhood in Persia — her family's house, the food she ate, the people she knew and the games she played — until she went to live in California with relatives at the age of nine because of danger during the First World War.

She also told me about her oldest sister, Susan, who went back to Persia in 1922, after the war was over, to be the director of an orphanage for Assyrian refugee children in Hamadan. The story of how Susan ran the orphanage and how she managed to help the children return to their own part of Persia was one of my favorites, and I thought that it should be made into a book.

I had a few letters written by Susan, by her stepmother who visited the orphanage, and by Mrs. McDowell, who worked with the Assyrian orphans when they were in Baghdad. And I had the stories that Susan had told my mother. There were also some newspaper articles about the journey made by the children. These gave me information about the orphanage and about the journey itself.

As I worked on *Home Is Beyond the Mountains*, I learned about the history and geography that had shaped the lives of the children before my Aunt Susan came to know them.

The History Behind the Story

The First World War lasted from 1914 to 1918. Turkey fought in the war on the side of Germany. For much of the war Turkey controlled the territory that is now the country of Iraq, to the south of present-day Turkey. The British fought against the Turkish army in this southern territory with the fighting spilling over into Persia east of Baghdad.

Although Persia was neutral in the war, Turkey invaded Persian territory in the north several times, hoping to take land. This made the position of the Assyrian villages that were near the Turkish border very dangerous.

The biggest invasion happened in the summer of 1918. So many Assyrian villages were destroyed and so many people killed that an estimated 80,000 Assyrians, along with many Armenians who lived in Persia, took whatever they could carry and fled, hoping to get behind the lines of the British army several hundred miles to the south. This was a very difficult journey, and about half the people who set out died on the way.

The British took responsibility for the refugees who came to them. They quickly built large camps using tents and equipment that were available because the war was actually coming to an end. One of the largest camps was at Baqubah, north of Baghdad.

Refugees arrived at the Baqubah camp in the late summer of 1918. The war ended just months later on November 11, 1918, but it took years for the details of the peace to be worked out. During this time the Assyrian refugees were not allowed to return to their homes. Many families and adults found ways to get to North America, Australia, Europe or other parts of the Middle

East, but many others, including the orphans, had to wait three years or more before they had a chance to return home.

In 1921 the orphans who had been in the Baqubah camp were among the first Assyrians allowed to go back to Persia. They were not sent to their villages in the north but to camps farther south. One was at Kermanshah. The Hamadan orphanage opened in 1922.

All of the cities, refugee camps and orphanages described in the novel are or were real places except for Samira and Benyamin's home village, Ayna. There were dozens of villages like Ayna scattered over the mountains, hills and plains between Lake Urmieh and the Turkish border.

Susan Shedd was, of course, a real person and so was Mrs. McDowell. All the other characters in the book are fictional.

Acknowledgments

Sorting out the family story, the Assyrian story and the historical background made this book challenging to write. I thank my editor, Shelley Tanaka, who patiently and insightfully took me through many rewrites, and my friend Joanne Schwartz, whose willingness to read and discuss successive drafts was both helpful and encouraging.